Mysteries of the

Ladybank Woods

*The unusual adventures of John and
Sandra*

C RICHARD TOYE

GREAT WESTERN BOOKS

Copyright © C Richard Toye 2009
First published in 2009 by Great Western Books
38 Abden Avenue, Kinghorn, Fife, Scotland, KY3 9TE
www.amolibros.co.uk

Distributed by Gardners Books, 1 Whittle Drive, Eastbourne,
East Sussex, BN23 6QH
Tel: +44(0)1323 521555 | Fax: +44(0)1323 521666

British Library Cataloguing in Publication Data
A catalogue record for this book is available from the British
Library.

ISBN 978-0-9543711-1-1

Typeset by Amolibros, Milverton, Somerset
This book production has been managed by Amolibros
Printed and bound by T J International Ltd, Padstow,
Cornwall, UK

The Author

Born in Plymouth, Devon, Charles Toye did a shipwright apprenticeship in Devonport and Rosyth Dockyards. He was in numerous managerial posts for the Ministry of Defence, one of which included a tour of duty in Gibraltar. He studied at Strathclyde University and gained a First Class Honours degree in Naval Architecture.

After two years as a marine surveyor for the Board of Trade at Belfast he returned to the MOD as a Naval Constructor at Rosyth Dockyard with duty at Swan Hunters Newcastle and finally at Rosyth Dockyard.

Previously published: *Sandy: the true story of a boy and his friends growing up in Cornwall in the late 1800s.*

Acknowledgements

I wish to thank the following for their help in the preparation of this book:

Staff of the public libraries of Kirkcaldy, Ladybank and Burntsland.

Mr Spital, Manager, Tay Forest District, of the Forestry Commission, Scotland.

Anne Weatherston.

This book is dedicated to my grandchildren James, Euan and Sarah Clayton. Their play during visits gave me some leads for certain parts of this book.

Contents

PART ONE

MYSTERIES OF THE LADYBANK WOODS

1

Problem with the house renovation

The Brown family lived in an old stone-built house near Dunfermline in the County of Fife. The family consisted of William Brown, a widower aged forty-five and his two children, John aged twelve and Sandra who was ten years old. Their mother Ruth had passed away two years before in 1979, after a long illness.

The only other person in the house was Mrs Forbes who was employed as a housekeeper and cook.

Fortunately, William Brown, being an engineer, was able to do much of his work at home. He was a man set in his ways and seemed older than his years. Although fond of his children he had difficulty in keeping them amused. But since his wife's illness he had neglected the upkeep of the house and it was now in need of a major renovation. The renovation would be extensive so it would require many of the rooms to be vacated and the furniture stored.

To overcome the problems this would cause, Mr Brown suggested to John and Sandra that while the building firm was working in the house they could stay with their Aunt Martha who lived in Ladybank, a small village about twenty miles from Dunfermline. So the best time to get the work done was in the summer school holidays.

John and Sandra were delighted with the suggestion as summer holidays could be boring and dull. Their previous stays with their aunt, although short, had been fun. She had made their stay interesting with trips up the coast to St Andrews and other seaside resorts. Most of all they enjoyed the picnics in the woods near her cottage.

With their agreement, Mr Brown wrote to his sister and asked if she would look after his children during the school holidays.

In her reply she said that she would be delighted to have John and Sandra to stay with her. Since her early retirement from the civil service she was looking for something to keep her active other than tending to her garden.

When the time came for their stay at Ladybank John and Sandra packed their clothes in readiness for the trip.

The next day their father took them in his Morris Minor, which was his pride and joy. The car, which he had bought new, was now twelve years old and he had looked after it for all those years. Being very fussy about the car, he even washed and polished it the day before the journey.

It took about an hour for the journey from Dunfermline to Ladybank for their father being a careful driver didn't go much over fifty m.p.h. They arrived in Ladybank early on the Saturday afternoon.

As Mr Brown drove into Ladybank he took the lower road to get to his sister's cottage. At the end of the lower road he approached the cottage which was at the end of a lane. The cottage was sited on a sloping bank and had large gardens at its back and front.

2

Aunt Martha welcomes the Brown family

As the car approached the cottage Mr Brown could see his sister at the garden gate waiting for them. Aunt Martha was the opposite to her brother, being tall and slim built. She kept herself fit by tending the gardens and taking long country walks.

At the gate Mr Brown and his children were warmly welcomed by their aunt. She let them into the cottage and showed John and Sandra their rooms, where they left their suitcases and came downstairs.

After the formalities of the children's stay had been settled between Mr Brown and his sister, they all sat down to a light meal. Not long after they had finished their meal Mr Brown said he had to leave. He had business to attend to and needed to return to Dunfermline.

After he had left John and Sandra went to their chosen rooms and unpacked their clothes. On their return downstairs Aunt Martha took them outside and showed them the changes she had made to the garden since their last visit.

After their walk around the garden the children remarked

to their aunt that they loved the gardens and the cottage. Their aunt since her early retirement had kept the gardens neat and tidy and had flowers in bloom all round the borders.

For several hours John and Sandra played in the back garden while their aunt did some sewing repairs to some of her clothes. Later Aunt Martha went indoors and worked in the kitchen. When she had finished and prepared some sandwiches she called John and Sandra in for supper.

After their supper the three of them retired to the front room for a while and chatted about a trip they could do the next day. By this time it was getting late in the evening and John and Sandra started to feel sleepy. Seeing this, Aunt Martha sent them off to their beds.

Although tired, John and Sandra didn't go to sleep right away, but spoke through the open doors of their rooms about all the adventures they hoped to enjoy in the next few weeks.

Little did they know that one of their adventures would lead to an unsuspecting turn of events.

3

John's find in the woods

The next day after breakfast their aunt suggested, as the weather was fine, that they should go for a walk in the lower woods, only a short walk from the cottage. As John and Sandra had been quite inactive the day before they were happy to agree.

When they arrived, the two children were surprised at the different types of trees growing there. After walking through the woods their aunt decided to sit on the grass in an open area while John and Sandra played hide and seek.

After a few minutes of playing John, who had been hiding, shouted to Sandra, "Come and see what I have found." Sandra walked over to where John was – in that part of the wood where the trees were quite old.

When she reached him he showed her, placed in the hollow of an old tree, a flat piece of slate. Lifting it out he showed her that there were markings on it. It looked as if the scratched markings showed a direction. Slowly he read out the scratched direction:

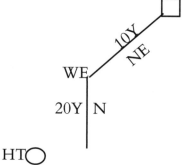

John and Sandra walked back to where their aunt was sitting and showed the slate to her. After she had a careful look at it she said, "It may be telling us where something was buried."

John and Sandra excitedly exclaimed, "It must be hidden treasure, maybe gold and silver coins."

Their aunt scolded them and told them not to jump to conclusions so quickly. "It must have been put there by children playing games. Anyway it is too late to look for any hiding place as we have to return to the cottage for our lunch. We'll have more time later to examine the slate and see if we can decipher the message."

After returning to the cottage the two children helped their aunt prepare the meal. They worked quickly as they were anxious to work out the message scratched on the slate.

As soon as they had finished their lunch the three of them sat down and examined their find. After pondering over the details on the slate their aunt said, "It looks to me as if the message is indicating the direction where whatever is hidden. The message seems to indicate that you go north from the hollow tree to the end of the wood. Then go on ten yards further to the north east."

John and Sandra jumped up excitedly from their chairs and asked their aunt, "May we go now and search for the treasure?"

She replied, "No! I have work to do in the cottage, we can search for your treasure tomorrow. Don't get any ideas that it is anything precious like gold or silver coins – as I said earlier it may have been left by children playing games."

Accepting their aunt's decision, John and Sandra offered to help with the housework. Aunt Martha was pleased with their offer and asked them to clean the rooms upstairs – John to vacuum the carpets while Sandra could clean the bathroom.

John and Sandra immediately set about their chores. Their aunt could tell they were busy because of the noise they were making upstairs. While they did their jobs Aunt Martha cleaned up the kitchen and then made preparations for the evening meal.

When John and Sandra had finished they came downstairs where their aunt was waiting for them with tea and cakes as a thank-you for all their hard work. After their tea they had a walk around the garden as the weather was still fine and warm.

On returning indoors Aunt Martha finished cooking the evening meal, while John and Sandra laid the table. After working hard upstairs John and Sandra were very hungry and when their aunt brought in the hot meal and dished it out they soon cleared their plates. As a special treat she brought in from the kitchen portions of hot apple tart with cream on top. Like the hot meal, they soon had their sweet eaten.

With their sweet finished, John and Sandra helped to

clear the table and wash the dishes. Afterwards the three of them retired to the front room. John and Sandra were now quite content to read the books they had brought with them, while Aunt Martha did some knitting on part of a jumper.

After reading their books for about an hour they started to get tired; their aunt, seeing this, sent them off to their rooms. After changing into their pyjamas they got into their beds. The finding of the slate with the message on it was still on their minds and they couldn't help talking about it. They expressed hopes that the message indicated where a treasure was buried. Soon they were too tired to talk any longer and fell asleep.

4

They search for the treasure

The next morning Aunt Martha took John and Sandra back to the lower woods. In her bag she carried a small spade and a compass.

They walked into the woods until they reached the hollow tree where John had found the slate. When they reached the tree Aunt Martha took out her compass. With this she took a direction north from the tree. The three of them then walked north through the woods until they reached the edge of the woods.

From this spot Aunt Martha used the compass to get a north-east direction, and then paced out ten yards as shown on the slate. When they reached the new spot where they expected the treasure to be buried they were taken aback at what they found. Around the area where they stood was a large outcrop of rock that would make it impossible for anything to be buried there.

John and Sandra were disappointed that they hadn't found any treasure. Their aunt seeing their disappointment said, "Never mind it was interesting trying to solve the mystery of the marked slate."

To cheer them up she said she would take them in her

car to St Andrews and spend the day there. So Aunt Martha returned with the children to the cottage. There they made up some sandwiches and cold drinks and with some fruit placed them in a picnic basket.

They loaded up the car with the basket, chairs and a blanket. When this was done their aunt drove off with John and Sandra in the back seat.

When they arrived at St Andrews their aunt parked the car near the long beach. They carried their basket, chairs and blanket to a grass area above the beach and laid out the food and drinks on the blanket.

As the three of them were hungry they soon tucked into the sandwiches and fruit. After their picnic they sat and watched people strolling along the beach and children playing in the sand making castles and other shapes.

Soon a small crowd gathered nearby. Sandra asked her aunt what they were looking at close to the beach. They were surprised to see people walking around with large cameras and clipboards. There seemed to be one man directing operations.

The three of them looked towards the area that the cameras were focusing on. It was a group of young men in running gear racing along the sand. Aunt Martha recognised some of the runners. She said to Sandra and John that being a film and television buff she could pick out from the group, Ben Cross, Ian Charleson and Nigel Havers who were famous actors.

"Can you believe it!" she said to John and Sandra. "They are making a film." The three of them watched the runners for a while racing across the sand, before they returned to their picnic area.

After some drinks Aunt Martha said they should have a walk before returning to Ladybank. So they packed their picnic things and took them up to the parking area and stowed them in the car. Then they walked along the road above the beach to the Old Golf Course Clubhouse. There they saw four golfers playing off on the first tee. After watching the golfers play on the famous "Old Course" for a while Aunt Martha said, "It's time to return home."

They strolled back to the car and Aunt Martha drove off to Ladybank. Naturally the conversation on the way home was all about seeing the film stars running on the beach and being there while the filming was taking place.

Later Aunt Martha found out that the actors were playing their parts in the film *Chariots of Fire*. The film was based on the true story of two members of Britain's 1924 Olympic competing team. Harold Abraham was a Jew running to prove himself in the face of the hostility he experienced in the British environment at that time. And Eric Liddell was a deeply religious man who refused to run on the Sabbath day in the Olympic Games in Paris.

On returning to the cottage at Ladybank the three of them were quite content after such a busy day to have a quiet evening after their evening meal.

5

Restricted to the cottage by the bad weather

With the weather turning from sunshine to heavy rain during the next day Aunt Martha decided they should stay near home for the next couple of days.

They only made short trips to buy groceries and newspapers at the local shops. When not tidying up and dusting in the cottage, Aunt Martha read the magazines she had purchased at the newsagent. John and Sandra played some card games but when they became bored playing cards Sandra went to her room to read her book *Lorna Doone*. While Sandra was absorbed in this dramatic story John stayed downstairs to help his aunt in the kitchen. After they had finished the preparation for the evening meal Aunt Martha and John sat down in the front room to relax.

Out of curiosity and because he was a person who liked solving puzzles John took down from the bookshelf, where it had been left, the marked slate he found in the hollow tree. He turned it around in different positions to see whether he had made a mistake with the directions shown on the slate of the supposed hiding place.

After puzzling over it for a while he put the slate back on the bookshelf. As he liked sitting with his aunt he went upstairs and fetched his book *Treasure Island*. He came down to the front room and read it for quite a long time. His aunt noticed he was quite absorbed in the book. She could imagine how John was fighting with the pirates on the treasure island in his thoughts.

After she had finished reading her magazines she asked John if he wanted a cool drink. He replied, "Yes please." As he had read for quite a long time he was glad to stop to have a drink. Aunt Martha shouted up to her niece, "Do you want a cool drink? I am making one up for John." Sandra having read her book for a long time too said, "Yes please" too and came downstairs.

When they had finished their drinks Aunt Martha suggested that they walk into Ladybank. As they had been cooped up all day John and Sandra were glad to get out. They walked around the village enjoying the warmth of the evening sunshine after all the rain.

They looked in the windows of the main street shops before Aunt Martha suggested that instead of the meal she had prepared she should buy fish and chips. John and Sandra whooped with delight at the suggestion and Aunt Martha walked them both down to the fish and chip shop at the end of the street.

On return to the cottage their aunt soon had the table laid for the fish and chips and some cool drinks. The walk had given them quite an appetite so all three of them enjoyed the unexpected meal.

After sitting in the front room for some time their aunt said that they should go to their beds early. She added that the weather was forecast to improve and she suggested that they get up early and visit South Queensferry the next day.

John and Sandra were all for another trip as they would be really bored if they stayed in the cottage for another day. They agreed with Aunt Martha's wishes and went to their beds early.

Aunt Martha after clearing up the kitchen sat in her favourite chair in the front room for a rest. She wasn't interested in watching television but picked up and started to read a book she had borrowed from the local library. After about half an hour she felt tired and went to her bed.

6

A Visit to South Queensferry

The next morning their aunt rose early and had a quick breakfast of tea and toast, then made up a picnic basket of sandwiches, cake, biscuits and cold drinks. When her preparations were complete she woke up John and Sandra and got their breakfast. The children helped clear the table and tidy the kitchen as soon as breakfast was over and were soon putting their coats and the picnic basket in the car.

As usual John and Sandra sat in the back of the car and Aunt Martha drove off. She decided to travel on the coastal route to South Queensferry. First she drove through Freuchie, known for its successful village cricket team and then bypassed the new town of Glenrothes.

Reaching the coast she drove through Dysart and then on to Kirkcaldy. Driving along the Kirkcaldy promenade they could see the spray from the sea coming over the sea wall. Aunt Martha told John and Sandra, "This usually happens when there is an onshore wind and the tide is high." She then drove through Kinghorn, Burntisland, Aberdour and Inverkeithing, finally to cross the Forth Road Bridge and down to South Queensferry. There she parked the car outside the Hawes Inn.

Before going into the inn she indicated to John and Sandra the sign hanging above one of the doors. On the sign was a picture of pirates wearing bandanas. John asked his aunt, "What is the link between the pirates' painting and the inn?" His aunt answered him saying, "The writer Robert Louis Stevenson in 1883 wrote part of his book *Treasure Island* in this inn – so the sign portrays this historical event."

After looking at the sign they went into the inn and Aunt Martha chose a quiet table in a corner of the lounge. Once settled they all selected something from the inn's menu after deciding to forego the picnic they had brought with them. This was soon served after the waiter had taken their order.

After their lunch the three of them walked down to the narrow beach in front of the inn. While John and Sandra picked up flat stones and played the skimming game on the water, Aunt Martha sat on a nearby seat and took in the view.

She was always enthralled to see how massive the railway bridge was, viewing it towering above her. She marvelled at the engineering skills of the men who built the cantilever bridge in the late 1800s. She compared the slim road bridge, close by, with the heavy girdered rail bridge and saw how different they were in their make-up. The road bridge suspended on multiple wires looked quite puny compared to the rail bridge.

Her thoughts wandered away to the Hawes Inn. She wondered if Robert Louis Stevenson had visited the Hawes Inn during the time that the railway bridge was being built.

Soon John and Sandra tired of playing on the beach

and came over to where Aunt Martha was sitting down. As it was late in the afternoon their aunt said it was time to go, especially as soon the bridge would be busy with commuters in their cars homeward bound from Edinburgh and Glasgow crossing the road bridge to Fife. They walked to the car and after settling John and Sandra in the back Aunt Martha drove off up the slope from the inn to the road bridge.

As the traffic was light, she was able to make good time driving across the bridge and along the coast road. As they reached Kirkcaldy Sandra asked her aunt about the long sea wall along the promenade. Her aunt explained that as there had been problems during storms with the flooding of houses opposite the promenade the local council decided to build a substantial sea wall. The building of the wall in the 1920s had two benefits, firstly it stopped the houses getting flooded and secondly it employed men who had been out of work for long periods after the First World War.

On leaving Kirkcaldy, Aunt Martha took the same coastal route back to Ladybank and arrived back at the cottage early in the evening.

As they had become dirty playing on the beach John and Sandra washed and changed their clothes. In the meantime their aunt prepared a meal of toasted sandwiches from the picnic basket with cakes and fruit to finish off.

After their meal John and Sandra fetched their books and sat down in the front room for a quiet evening of reading. Sandra was only halfway through *Lorna Doone*, but John had nearly finished *Treasure Island*.

Aunt Martha, looking at John with affection, and seeing

that he was completely absorbed in the book, imagined that he was living the part of Jim Hawkins the hero of the book. Within an hour John had finished the last chapters of the book. When his aunt looked at him John said to her, "The end of the story was quite exciting, especially with the pirates and Long John Silver being besieged in the stockade on the treasure island."

As it was now getting late in the evening Aunt Martha said to John and Sandra, "You've had a long day, it's time to go to your beds now." Once they had gone to their bedrooms Aunt Martha tidied up the kitchen and washed the crockery and utensils that were used for their supper. After watching the news programme on the television she went to her own room upstairs.

About an hour later while she was sleeping a sudden cry woke her. Realising that the cry came from John in his bedroom, she put on her dressing gown and rushed across. As she opened the door John cried out again, waking Sandra as well this time. Within seconds she joined her aunt to see what the matter was.

In the bedroom they could see that John was now wide awake, and sitting up. Aunt Martha asked him what was wrong to make him cry out and John told her, "I had a terrible dream. In the dream I was being chased by ugly-looking pirates. At first I was able to run away from them but then my legs wouldn't move and the pirates were catching up on me. When they came close to me I cried out and woke up."

Aunt Martha smiled. "You've had a bad dream after becoming too absorbed in your *Treasure Island* book. The characters in the story must be have become almost real to you, and that's what's caused you to have a bad dream. Still no harm's been done. I'll bring you up a mug of hot chocolate which should help you to have a calm sleep." Not long after John had finished his drink he was fast asleep.

For the rest of the night the cottage was quiet and John woke up the next morning without any more bad dreams about pirates chasing him. On coming downstairs the three of them had a good laugh about John's nightmare.

After breakfast Aunt Martha asked John and Sandra if they would like to go to the Fair at Burntisland. Without hesitation John and Sandra said, "Yes please!" Aunt Martha, pleased with their instant and eager reply, said they should set out after they had been to the shops at Ladybank to buy some groceries.

7

A trip to the Fair at Burntisland

On their return from the shops the three of them prepared food and drinks for the trip. With the preparations complete, John and Sandra loaded up the car with the picnic basket and a blanket to sit on. With John and Sandra settled in the back of the car, Aunt Martha drove off on the road to Freuchie and then on to Dysart and the coast road.

Along the coast road she stopped at a memorial created just outside Kinghorn on the Burntisland road. John asked his aunt "Why are we stopping here?"

His aunt replied, "If you get out of the car I will show you something that might interest you." The three of them walked to the memorial on which Aunt Martha indicated a plaque. The plaque commemorated the place where Alexander III King of Scots fell off his horse down the cliff to his death in 1286 while returning from Edinburgh to his castle in Kinghorn.

She explained to John and Sandra that the death of this king had a dramatic effect on the history of Scotland. She went on to say that Alexander's only heir to the throne was a grand-daughter the 'Maid of Norway', Margaret, but she died on her voyage from Norway to Scotland. On her death there were many claimants for the throne which caused numerous battles and bloodshed. It culminated in Robert the Bruce becoming King of Scots. The kingship settled with Bruce defeating the English army under King Edward II at Bannockburn in 1314.

After looking over the cliff where Alexander might have fallen from his horse the three of them returned to the car.

Aunt Martha drove on to the Fair in Burntisland which was only about a mile further on from the monument. There she parked the car at the back of the 'Links' near the railway line.

They walked from the car to a grassy slope away from the Fair. Their aunt set out the picnic items on the blanket they had brought with them so that they could eat before going to it.

While they were enjoying their picnic John who was always inquisitive asked his aunt, "How did Burntisland get its name?"

In reply his aunt explained that a local historian told her the origin of the name Burntisland was unclear as no one is sure how the town got its name. The most recited version of the name is that the green island, which was later excavated to build the harbour, was where fishermen's huts and outbuildings were destroyed by fire, hence the name 'Burnt Island'.

When they had finished their picnic Aunt Martha and Sandra tidied up the area they were sitting on before packing up the picnic basket. As it was only a short walk to the car John volunteered to take the basket and blanket there. On his return he walked with Sandra and his aunt to the entrance to the Fair.

After looking at some of the stalls Sandra had several goes at the hoopla and won a small teddy bear. John didn't seem to have any luck, as after many goes at the coconut shy he couldn't knock one over. When they'd had enough of the stalls John and Sandra paid for a mat each and slid down the helter skelter several times.

Next John and Sandra paid to have a go on a boat swing. They climbed in the boat and, with both of them pulling on the ropes, worked up a reasonable speed. This didn't satisfy John as he wanted to go faster and higher, and tried to show off his strength by pulling hard at the ropes to get the boat to go higher. Despite his efforts the boatswing would only go to a certain height and speed. By the time he had stopped his efforts John was red in the face and gasping for breath. Sandra couldn't contain herself and just roared with laughter to see him in such a state. After John had recovered his breath he walked with Sandra back to where Aunt Martha was waiting for them nearby. She had seen John's antics in the boatswing but only smiled and didn't say anything about it when they reached her.

Aunt Martha asked if they had enough of the Fair. Both said they had, and had enjoyed the amusements and stalls they had chosen so were quite happy to go back to the cottage. John declared, "I'm really tired after all my efforts on the boatswing!"

Aunt Martha and Sandra looked at each other and smiled at John's outburst. They had to stop themselves from laughing at him. They soon walked to the car which was parked close by and their aunt drove them back to the cottage.

Once home, Aunt Martha asked John and Sandra to

wash and get changed. By the time they had returned downstairs their aunt served up a hot meal which she had prepared the previous day.

After the meal the three of them cleared up and washed and dried the dishes. This done the three of them retired to the front room where they were content to read their books.

After a while John picked up the marked slate he found in the hollow tree, to look at it again to see if there were any more score marks on the slate. He was hoping that finding more marks would show a different direction for finding the treasure. He soon became tired of looking at the slate and put it back on the shelf.

Later in the evening Aunt Martha said that as it had been a long day they should go to their beds. As they were tired John and Sandra didn't object to going to bed and they soon went up to their rooms.

Their aunt did some tidying up, but then went upstairs to her bedroom. Before going into her room she looked in on John and Sandra and found them fast asleep. Quite content, she went to her bed and was soon asleep herself.

8

John and Sandra help in the garden

The next day Aunt Martha said to John and Sandra, "I have to catch up on work in the garden so instead of going on a trip would you help me out there?" John and Sandra said that they'd had enough of travelling for the time being and would like to help.

So the three of them went into the garden where their aunt showed John and Sandra where some weeding was needed in one of the flowerbeds. While Aunt Martha did some pruning of bushes, John and Sandra did some weeding at the bottom of the garden.

After about an hour John and Sandra had lifted enough weeds to fill the light wheelbarrow that Aunt Martha had brought down to them. They filled it up and John took it up to the compost heap at the top of the garden and threw the weeds on the top of the heap. On his return, as they had finished the weeding he suggested to Sandra that he take her for a ride in the wheelbarrow. Not thinking there would be any harm in it she readily accepted.

Sandra was quite happy to be pushed around the garden by John. After pushing Sandra around for a short while John ran fast with her in the wheelbarrow to the top of the garden. When she least expected it John dumped her on the compost heap.

Sandra was quite angry at first as her hair and clothes were covered in rotted grass and weeds. Worst of all she smelt of rotten vegetation. She brushed herself down and yelled at him, "I will get even with you, John."

Aunt Martha who was walking up from the bottom of the garden had to hide a smile at what had happened. She said to John, "That was naughty of you, John, you will have to apologise to Sandra."

John said to Sandra, "I am sorry but it was only a bit of fun."

Sandra replied, "I didn't think it was funny especially as your prank has messed up my clothes."

Aunt Martha took the matter in hand and calmed Sandra down and told her to go inside to wash and change. She turned to John and said, "You'll have to get washed and changed as well."

While John and Sandra were washing and changing their clothes, Aunt Martha prepared some cool drinks for them and cut some cake. On coming downstairs, John and Sandra soon tucked into the cake and drinks as they were quite thirsty and hungry after the weeding in the garden.

Afterwards Aunt Martha asked them if they would like a trip to a friend near Ladybank. She had to return some magazines to her but they could stop on the way back and buy some ice creams in the general shop in the main street. John and Sandra said they would like that very much, especially as they would be getting some ice creams.

So in the afternoon Aunt Martha brought the car out from the garage and, with John and Sandra ready for once, she drove them off to her friend's house.

After returning the magazines to her friend, only stopping for a chat on the doorstep, she went back to the car, where John and Sandra were anxiously waiting for her, glad that she hadn't had a long conversation with her friend. Without any more delay they drove back to the Main Street in Ladybank.

It was only a short walk to the main shopping area so John and Sandra didn't have long to wait before they reached the shop selling the ice cream. John and Sandra asked for cones and were all eyes when Aunt Martha appeared from the shop with large ice cream cones, adorned with chocolate flake sticks. As there was a seat outside the shop John and Sandra ate their ice cream before returning to the car.

9

Sandra finds a young hare

On their return to the cottage, while Aunt Martha was driving the car into the garage, John and Sandra waited for her at the garden gate. As their aunt seemed to be a long time in the garage, Sandra walked along the front of the garden. As she looked towards the Lower Woods she noticed what seemed to be a bundle of fur in the gutter.

She walked up to it and noticed it was an animal crouching against the kerb. Sandra, seeing it more clearly, shouted to her aunt who was just unlocking the front door, "It's a little rabbit, Aunt, and seems to be hurt."

Aunt Martha and John, curious about the animal, walked quickly to where Sandra was standing. Their aunt looked at the animal and recognised it although it was hunched up in a ball. She told Sandra, "It's not a rabbit it's a small hare."

She picked it up and found out that it was still alive, though its eyes were half closed. The three of them took the hare into the cottage and put it in a large cardboard box in the warmest part of the kitchen.

She gave the hare some water and loose corn from a packet in one of the cupboards. After eating the corn and drinking the water the animal became more lively and started to move around the box. John and Sandra were fascinated with the little hare. It was silver-grey in colour and its fur seemed to shine in the sunlight. John and Sandra hadn't seen a hare in the wild before and were amazed at how long its ears and legs were for such a small animal.

After watching the young hare move around the box for some time Sandra asked her aunt what they should do with it. Aunt Martha replied, "I have a friend who is a veterinary surgeon and we'll take the hare to him to see if it is hurt in any way."

The next morning Aunt Martha woke up John and Sandra early, after preparing breakfast for them. Over breakfast she told them that after they had finished they could take the hare to the vet. The vet was called James Fleming and he had a surgery in Kirkcaldy. As she didn't have a telephone they would have to visit the surgery and hope to catch him before his first appointment.

When she had finished breakfast Sandra gave the hare some water and lettuce. The hare seemed quite lively after being in the warm kitchen overnight. After clearing up in the kitchen Aunt Martha brought out the car and as usual John and Sandra jumped into the back seat.

The journey didn't take long and soon they were in Kirkcaldy where their aunt parked the car close to the vet's surgery. Aunt Martha had timed the visit to reach the surgery just before the start of Mr Fleming's surgery hours. With Sandra carrying the box with the hare in it the three of them entered the surgery. They were lucky to catch Mr Fleming right away. As they entered his office he was examining his appointments list for the day.

He turned around on their entry and saw Aunt Martha and smiled in recognition and said, "I'm pleased to see you after such a long time. How are you enjoying your sojourn at your cottage in Ladybank?" (Their aunt had moved to Ladybank after early retirement from her job in Kirkcaldy.) Aunt Martha replied, "Fine, thank you, I'm enjoying my retirement."

After John and Sandra were introduced to Mr Fleming by Aunt Martha he asked her, "What can I do for you?" Aunt Martha told him, "My niece has found a small hare near my cottage. We took the animal into the cottage as we thought it had either been hurt by a fall or had been hit by a passing vehicle."

Mr Fleming invited the three of them into his surgery. There he took the hare out of the box and placed it on the operating table. After his examination he said to Aunt Martha, "I can't find anything wrong with the hare," and put it back in the box. He advised her that they should keep the hare inside for one more day to make sure it was fit enough to go back into the wild again. He added, "You shouldn't keep the hare any longer as it could become domesticated and then not be able to fend for itself in the wild. By the way there will be no charge for the examination."

Aunt Martha thanked him for his help and went out with John and Sandra to the car. The journey to the cottage was quite pleasant as the weather was warm and sunny. John and Sandra in the back seat could only talk about the hare.

On their return to the cottage John and Sandra gave the hare some water and lettuce. For the rest of the day they had to make constant trips to the kitchen to see the hare. Aunt Martha soon realised that John and Sandra were getting attached to the little creature.

With John and Sandra going to bed early that evening Aunt Martha had a quiet hour to herself sitting reading in the front room. Before going to bed herself she thought if they kept the hare much longer she was sure John and Sandra would try to persuade her to keep it indefinitely, so for the hare's sake this should not happen.

10

The hare is let loose in the woods

The next day after breakfast, seeing that the hare was quite lively and recovered from its hurt, Aunt Martha firmly told John and Sandra that they should take the hare to the woods. So they all went with the young hare in the box to the edge of the woods.

When they reached the woods Sandra chose a suitable clear area between the nearest trees and opened up the box. She let the young hare down onto the ground clear of the box. After snuffling around in the grass the hare suddenly scampered out into the wooded area and was soon out of sight.

Curious about what would happen to the hare, Sandra asked her aunt, "Will the hare find its original burrow all right?"

Her aunt told her, "Hares don't live in burrows. Hopefully the young hare will find its nest above ground hidden below bushes in the woods."

When Aunt Martha looked at the faces of John and Sandra she knew they were sad that they had to let the hare go back to the woods. To cheer them up and help them get over the loss of the animal when they returned to the cottage their aunt cooked them their favourite meal of fish and chips for that evening.

11

They visit Aunt Martha's friend

The three of them had a quiet couple of days at the weekend with only house cleaning and laundering to be done. It suited John and Sandra to help Aunt Martha indoors as the weather was poor with regular showers occurring each day.

On the Sunday the sun came out and the weather forecast was good. Aunt Martha asked John and Sandra if they would like to take a walk to Giffordtown, about two miles away. She had promised a friend who lived there that she would take her some plants from the garden. They could walk through the Lower Woods on the way back and look for the young hare that they cared for and released there.

As the day was sunny the three of them enjoyed the walk to their aunt's friend's home in Giffordtown. On their arrival at the house they were greeted at the door by Mrs Neil and invited in.

After handing over the plants to her friend Aunt Martha introduced John and Sandra to her. Mrs Neil asked John and Sandra how they were enjoying their holiday with their aunt. They both said that they were enjoying their holiday, especially being able to visit so many interesting places in the area. After they had been chatting for a while Mrs Neil made some tea and brought out some very large cream cakes which John and Sandra goggled at hungrily. It didn't take John and Sandra very long to make short work of them, although as usual John ended up with plenty of cream on his face.

With their tea and cakes finished, the conversation continued with John and Sandra telling Mrs Neil how they had found a young hare and also discovered the marked slate that had been placed in a hollow tree in the woods.

Mrs Neil said to Aunt Martha, "You should be careful about going through the woods especially in the evening. There has been some queer goings-on in the woods of late. Only recently someone was robbed as they walked through the woods on their way to Ladybank. And there was a mysterious happening occurred in these woods years ago. A tale has been told of a weaver in the 1800s who had been moved with other villagers from Kinloch to Monkestown in the vicinity of Ladybank. He was returning through the Lower Woods to his home and never came out of the woods alive and lost his life in a strange way.

"It was a dark night with heavy rain and he stumbled and fell into a bog and drowned. Some of the folk at the time thought he could have been deliberately drowned by local weavers who were jealous of his success in selling his wares. From the time of his drowning the villagers round about said that his ghost walks through the woods on rainy days."

Aunt Martha after hearing Mrs Neil recounting the tale

said, "I can't understand how the weaver fell into a bog and drowned. The woods seem mainly dry to me."

Mrs Neil replied, "Yes, the woods are mainly dry now but in the 1500s a large bog in the woods did exist. In fact the original name for Ladybank was given as 'Our Lady's Bog' by the first monk of Lindores Abbey nearby. In later years the gentry hereabouts decided to change the name to Ladybank. With the draining of the surrounding fields in the area the ground in the woods became dry."

So half-joking she said, "You will have to avoid the woods on a rainy day."

Aunt Martha replied, "As regards the possibility of being robbed when going through the woods I always take my heavy walking stick with me to defend myself if ever I got waylaid."

As time was passing John and Sandra were getting restless. Aunt Martha seeing this said to Mrs Neil, "We must be off. Despite the ghost we want to walk through the woods and look for the young hare we cared for last week."

John and Sandra thanked Mrs Neil for the tea and cream cakes and, saying their goodbyes, they were soon walking towards the woods.

On reaching the woods they took the main path through it. Further into the woods they passed the hollow tree. John asked his aunt if he could check the position marked on the slate of the hidden treasure, as he had memorised the markings.

Aunt Martha after hesitating, thinking it wasn't worthwhile, reluctantly gave in and let John pace out the directions marked on the slate. At the end of his pacing he still ended up at the large outcrop of rock. He was quite dejected: after all, his hopes were dashed for the second time of still not finding the treasure.

Aunt Martha, to cheer him up said, "Come on, I think I may know where your young hare could be living in the wood. There is a high bank on the south side of the wood where it is likely a hare's nest could be found."

John perked up with his aunt's suggestion so the three of them continued to walk through the wood. After walking for a few minutes Sandra stopped and said to her aunt, "I thought I heard someone following us. I heard twigs being broken nearby and I saw a shape of a man in the faraway bushes." Aunt Martha looked in the direction pointed out by Sandra, but couldn't see or hear anything of an intruder watching them.

Putting aside the thought of being followed, they walked on to the south side of the wood. There they approached the high bank quietly and started looking for the hare's nest. After searching for a while Sandra found a nest deep in the undergrowth. All of a sudden a hare jumped out of the bushes near the nest, which startled the three of them. While they were standing still, after the surprise of seeing it, the hare looked at them for a moment and then scampered off further into the bushes.

Sandra, recovering from the surprise, said, "That hare looked like the little one we befriended."

Aunt Martha smiled: "I doubt if we will ever find out if it was that one as they are very shy animals and we were lucky to get that close to the little hare. Although I must admit it did look like our little hare."

After all the excitement of seeing the hare they climbed down from the bank and rejoined the main path to walk out of the wood. Their aunt, as they came out of the wood, told them, "I think that's enough excitement for one day. We shall go back to the cottage and prepare a meal for this evening. By the way, John, I don't want you dreaming tonight of the ghost of the weaver walking through the woods."

The three of them laughed at the comment, but Sandra was still thinking about someone who had followed them in the wood as they returned to the cottage.

12

A trip to Crail and a boy is hurt in a fall

With the weather keeping fine the next day, Aunt Martha suggested to John and Sandra that they take a trip to Crail for the day. John and Sandra said they last visited Crail with their parents many years ago. John remembered playing on the beach there and was keen to go again.

Aunt Martha said, "That's good as it is one of my favourite places in Fife to visit. We should prepare a picnic basket for our day out." So the three of them set to and made up sandwiches and cool drinks. Aunt Martha cut up a large cake and put it in the basket as well as some fruit.

While she was bringing out the car from the garage John and Sandra brought out the picnic basket. While Aunt Martha fetched a windbreak from the back of the garage John and Sandra loaded up the car. Their aunt put the windbreak in the car, telling John and Sandra, "The windbreak will come in handy as it can be quite windy on the beach at Crail."

As soon as this was done John and Sandra jumped into the back of the car. Once they were settled in Aunt Martha drove off and headed for Crail.

She went by the coast road as it was a pleasanter drive going through Pittenweem and Anstruther before reaching Crail. On their arrival at Crail their aunt parked near the main street so that they could walk down to the old harbour. They strolled along it, looking in the shops, then went on down to the harbour where they looked at the numerous fishing boats berthed alongside the inner walls. John and Sandra were captivated with the different shapes and colours of the fishing boats and their curious names.

While walking around, they could see several persons with easels or boards painting pictures of the quaint stone harbour nestling into the hillside. Some of the paintings looked very colourful and captured the quaintness of the harbour scene.

After walking back to the car Aunt Martha drove them to the car parking area just above and beyond Crail. John and Sandra soon unloaded the car and took the picnic basket and windbreak down to where their aunt had picked out a suitable quiet spot away from other families using the beach.

Once the windbreak had been secured into the sand John and Sandra laid out the food and drink on the blanket placed inside it. As it had been several hours since they had their breakfast the three of them soon tucked into the picnic. After the meal John and Sandra played on the beach while Aunt Martha read a book. Sandra quickly became tired of playing and joined her aunt sitting inside the windbreak.

John told his aunt that he wanted to explore the area and she warned him, "Don't go too far away and stay away from the high cliff at the end of the beach. It's dangerous because it has loose rocks on its face that keep falling down onto the beach."

John nodded his head in agreement and strolled along the beach picking up colourful shells. As he reached the end of the beach he saw that the area beyond the end of the beach was roped off with a notice stating DANGEROUS CLIFF WITH FALLING ROCK. Looking up at the cliff he was startled to see a boy about his own age trying to climb up the cliff. Just as the boy reached the top he slipped and fell. He landed on a ledge halfway down the cliff and cried out, "I've hurt my leg and I can't move." John, seeing that the boy was hurt and stranded on the ledge ran back to his aunt and told her what had happened. Aunt Martha knowing the locality told John to run to the cottage above the beach as she knew it was occupied by a local fisherman.

John ran up the bank from the beach and knocked at the cottage door. The fisherman who thankfully was at home at the time opened the door and asked him what he wanted. He could see that John was distressed and out of breath after running all the way up from the beach. John blurted out, "A boy has fallen down the cliff onto a ledge and seems badly hurt; will you help to rescue him please?"

The fisherman knowing the cliff was dangerous said to John, "I'll just fetch two ropes from my shed and go down to the beach with you."

On his return the fisherman walked with John to the beach where he was met by Aunt Martha and a man who explained to the fisherman that he was the father of the boy trapped on the cliff. He had telephoned for an ambulance from one of the houses above the beach his family had been renting while on holiday at Crail.

The fisherman seeing the worry on the father's face said, "Don't worry, I'll get your boy down safely." He went on to say "I'll lower myself with a rope from the top of the cliff on to the ledge, then tie the second rope on to your son and lower him slowly down to the beach. If you stand at the bottom of the cliff, you can support your boy before he reaches the ground."

Nervous, but accepting what the fisherman said he would do to save his son, the man made his way to the bottom of the cliff and stood in line with the ledge high above him.

In the meantime the fisherman with his ropes climbed up the high bank above the beach to get to the top of the cliff. When he reached the top of the bank he walked to the edge of the cliff to see where the boy was on the ledge. Then he tied the end of one rope to a stone pillar that was sturdy enough to take his weight and lowered the rope over the cliff to the ledge. He wrapped the other rope around his waist and then gradually, using the first rope, climbed down the cliff slowly to the ledge. He was very careful to avoid dislodging any loose rocks on his way down. On reaching the ledge he checked the condition of the boy and found he was breathing normally but was bleeding from some cuts. Then he asked the boy about his leg and was told it was quite painful. After a look at the leg the fisherman said, "It looks as if it's broken so I'll be careful as I lower you down to the beach."

He then unwrapped the rope from his waist and tied the end under the boy's arms. After signalling to the boy's father below, the fisherman lowered the casualty on the rope slowly to the beach where his father caught him. Then he lowered his son slowly onto the beach and freed him from the rope.

After wrapping the freed rope around himself the fisherman climbed back to the top of the cliff and untied the other rope from the pillar. He coiled up the two ropes and made his way down to the beach.

By the time the fisherman had reached the beach the boy's father had washed the blood off his son's face and arms and covered him in a blanket to keep him warm and avoid any shock as a result of the fall. He thanked the fisherman for rescuing his son.

Soon afterwards the ambulance arrived at the road above the beach. Quite quickly the attendants of the ambulance brought down a stretcher and soon had the injured boy strapped into it, with splints on his broken leg. They took him up to the ambulance and made him comfortable for the journey to the hospital. Quite anxious about his son's condition, the father went with the ambulance to the hospital. Aunt Martha added her thanks to the fisherman before he returned to his cottage. She returned to the windbreak where John and Sandra had been watching the rescuing of the injured boy. She told them, "That's enough excitement for today – we should pick up our things and return home."

John and Sandra gathered up the picnic items and lifted out the windbreak and took them up to the car parked above the beach. After checking her exit as the road was narrow and there were many parked cars in front of them, Aunt Martha drove off. She took a more direct route back to Ladybank through Cupar. With little traffic on the road they returned to the cottage in about an hour.

Back at the cottage John and Sandra unloaded the car and took the picnic things into the cottage while Aunt Martha garaged the car.

As it was now quite late in the day Aunt Martha made up a quick meal of scrambled egg on toast. As it had been some time since their picnic, John and Sandra soon ate their meal with mugs of tea to wash it down. After clearing up when their meal was finished John and Sandra fetched their books to read while their aunt made herself comfortable with a magazine she had recently purchased.

After about half an hour John became bored with reading and went over to the bookshelf and picked up the marked slate from the hollow tree. For a while he pondered over the markings on the slate.

As she had finished reading her magazine, Aunt Martha asked John and Sandra if they would like some lemonade. They both said, "Yes please," as they were thirsty and also because the lemonade was home-made by Aunt Martha and had a delicious flavour.

While he was drinking his lemonade John spilt some of his lemonade onto the slate. The liquid formed a bubble over the markings, making them much clearer. "Aunt Martha, Aunt Martha!" exclaimed John. "There are other markings on the slate we didn't see before."

She came over with Sandra, both curious at his outburst, and looked at the slate. They could see the missed markings more clearly under the liquid. Aunt Martha was pleased: "I shall get some chalk and rub it into the markings which should show them up more clearly." She went to a drawer and picked out some chalk and carefully rubbed it on to the marked area.

As John had discovered it did show up the missed markings scored on the slate.

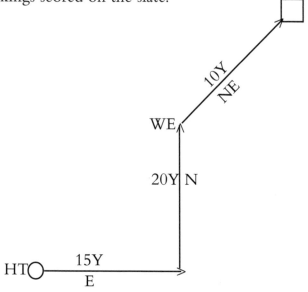

Aunt Martha after examining the markings more closely said she agreed with John that they had missed these other markings. She added, "It now shows that we should have first taken a direction fifteen yards easterly before going in a northerly direction. This would have taken us to a position clear of the outcrop of rock. Tomorrow we will go to the woods and pace out the correct directions. This time, John, you may find your hidden treasure.

John and Sandra were both excited at the prospect of finding the hidden treasure. Aunt Martha calmed them down and said, "Don't get your hopes up yet. Just let us see what we discover tomorrow."

Later in the evening John and Sandra said they were

tired and would go to their beds. Despite their tiredness they were still talking about the hidden treasure as they went upstairs.

13

They find the treasure in the woods

The next morning, while John and Sandra were eating their breakfast, Aunt Martha, as she didn't have a telephone in the cottage, walked down the road to a public telephone box and rang the hospital where the injured boy had been taken. The duty nurse told her that the boy had a quiet night and was recovering quite well. He would be in for a few days to make sure the bone was setting properly in its cast, as it was quite a bad break. On her return to the cottage she related to John and Sandra how the injured boy was faring in the hospital.

When John and Sandra had finished their breakfast and tidied up the kitchen, she said, "Get your coats and I will find my compass and fetch a spade from the shed. We are going to the wood to search for your hidden treasure."

John and Sandra couldn't get their coats on quick enough for their walk to the woods to check the position of the treasure from the markings on the slate. It didn't take them long to walk there as John set off at a brisk pace. On reaching the wood they made their way to the hollow tree where John had found the slate.

At the hollow tree John paced out the newly found

directions from the slate and ended up at a small clearing near the end of the wood. There John discovered a spot where the grass had recently been disturbed. He dug out the turf, and earth to a depth of about a foot. As he continued to dig he hit something hard with the spade.

Clearing the last of the earth John found a rectangular-shaped object wrapped in sacking. He lifted it out and unwrapped the sacking. Inside the sacking was a beautifully ornamental casket. Aunt Martha looked at the casket and said to John and Sandra, "This casket is very old and could even be medieval."

John opened the casket and found inside some parchments. Aunt Martha on a closer inspection said, "The writing on these parchments are in Latin." She added, "I have a friend in Cupar called John Reid who is a local historian. We could take it to him and he may be able to tell us about its origin."

By chance John looked in the hole just before he was going to fill it in. At the bottom he saw a slate similar to the one he found in the hollow tree. Although it was dirty he lifted it out before filling in the hole and replacing the turf. He placed the slate on top of the rewrapped casket and with his aunt and sister made his way back to the cottage.

Later that day Aunt Martha telephoned the historian John Reid. When he was given the details of the casket he said that he was quite keen to see it. He invited her and her kin to his home in Cupar for the Friday evening when he could be home early from his office.

14

The Historian examines the casket

On the Friday Aunt Martha, with John and Sandra, drove to John Reid's home in Cupar. When they arrived they were made most welcome. After some conversation about Aunt Martha's retirement to her cottage after ceasing employment in Kirkcaldy, she unwrapped the casket from the sacking for John Reid to examine it and the parchments inside.

He carefully inspected the casket and parchments and said, "You were right in saying it was medieval. I saw a similar casket to this at Falkland Palace about a year ago. Could you leave it with me and I will try to investigate its origin?"

Aunt Martha said, "Yes please. I hope it won't give you too much trouble."

"Not at all," replied John Reid. "I will try to get you an answer fairly quickly."

After John Reid had given them some tea and biscuits they left and returned to the cottage. On their return the three of them settled down to a quiet evening just reading books in the front room.

John after a short while, being an inquisitive person,

closed his book and took down the dirty slate from the bookshelf where it had been placed. He fetched a rag from the kitchen and with much effort cleaned off the dirt. To his joy there on the slate was scored another set of markings giving directions. These were:

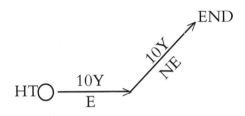

He jumped up and shouted. "There's another treasure hidden in the woods."

Aunt Martha and Sandra came over to where John was dancing around and calmed him down. Aunt Martha took some chalk out of a drawer and carefully covered the area of the markings on the slate. After close examination of the slate their aunt said, "It seems there are only two directions scored on the slate and no others. At least the chalk doesn't show any other markings on the slate. The markings look like a message similar to the one on the other slate." She added, "Don't get your hopes up, John. It may not be meant as a message for the hiding of a treasure. Let us check it out in the woods tomorrow."

15

John finds the hidden treasure

The following morning John and Sandra got up early for their breakfast. They were quite excited at the prospect of looking for hidden treasure again but remembering their previous attempt at using the first slate's markings they were not confident of finding anything. It was more in hope that they would be able to find the place marked on the slate.

Once they had cleared up after breakfast John and Sandra couldn't get out of the cottage quick enough. Aunt Martha had to smile at their urgency as they strode out in their walk from the cottage to the wood. When they reached the spot where the casket had been buried John took the second slate out of his pocket.

He paced out the directions marked on the slate and found a spot where again the turf had been recently dug up. John lifted the turf with the spade and dug down about six inches. He stopped as he could see the top of some sacking. He cleared the earth from the sacking and lifted it out. The sacking was wrapped around another soft bag. When John unwrapped the sacking he found inside a black bag. Opening the bag he was astonished to see in it a diamond-studded necklace, brooches, bracelets and other items of jewellery. The precious stones on the jewellery shone in the sunlight.

Sandra and Aunt Martha came closer and looked at the large amount of jewellery in amazement. "My gosh!" exclaimed their aunt as she took in the variety of valuables in the bag. "I must say that I think these jewels have been stolen. We must take them to the police right away."

John first tied the bag of jewels and wrapped it in the sacking then started to fill in the hole. As he was filling in the hole John noticed a man was watching them from the nearby bushes. "Look!" cried John, pointing the man out to his aunt and Sandra. Getting a better look at the stranger, they noticed he was heavily built with a large head, his face heavily jowled. His hair was short and spiky.

The stranger came out of the bushes and came striding towards them but stopped as a man and a woman appeared, coming along a nearby path. When he saw them the stranger turned quickly and made for the bushes. He was gone before the three could do anything to discover what the stranger wanted from them. Recovering, Aunt Martha said, "If I am not mistaken that may have been the thief who buried the jewels. We must take the stolen jewellery to the police right away."

John quickly filled in the hole, and holding the wrapped bag under his arm walked with his aunt and sister out of the woods. As soon as they reached the cottage Aunt Martha fetched the car keys and brought the car out of the garage. With John and Sandra quickly jumping in the back their aunt drove off to the police station.

At the police station their aunt handed the bag of stolen

jewellery to the policeman on duty. She explained to the constable the circumstances of how they came to dig up the bag. She added that there had been a man watching them dig up the stolen jewellery. The man had looked when he approached them as if he was going to accost them, but was disturbed by people walking along nearby in the woods.

The policeman asked Aunt Martha to write out a statement of the circumstances of finding the stolen jewellery. This she did and handed it over to him. The constable called his sergeant in and explained the details of her statement to him. The sergeant said to her, "This is a dangerous situation for you and the children. Here is my card with my telephone number on it. If you are approached by this man, telephone me right away. We will apprehend the man and take him in for questioning about the theft of the jewellery." Their aunt said she would do as he asked and thanked him and the constable for their help in the matter.

16

*They return to the cottage and
have a surprise visitor*

Aunt Martha, with John and Sandra excitedly talking in
the back about the finding of the jewellery, drove back
to the cottage. As soon as the car was put away the three
of them, after a quick look around, went into to the cottage.
Aunt Martha locked up the doors and windows in the
cottage in case the stranger they'd seen approaching them
in the wood was lurking in the area. After a while calm
returned to the home and Aunt Martha prepared a meal
for the three of them. They all ate the meal heartily as
their last meal had been their early breakfast many hours
ago. After their meal the three of them settled down in
the front room for a quiet evening.

Although Aunt Martha tried to keep the conversation
away from the subject of the stolen jewellery, John and
Sandra kept returning to the subject and the scare they'd
had at the approach of the ugly man in the woods.

To distract John and Sandra from their conversation on
the stolen jewellery their aunt switched on the television as
there was a good programme that would suit them. About
halfway through it there was a knock at the door and then

further loud knocks. This startled them as they thought this might be the man who had been watching them in the woods and who might have found out where they lived. Tentatively Aunt Martha went to the door and opened it only partly with a chain holding the door.

She was pleasantly surprised to see Mr Reid the historian standing there. "Please come in, Mr Reid," she said with some relief in her voice. He came into the cottage holding the wrapped-up casket. When she had settled him down in the front room he said good evening to John and Sandra. "I wish to explain why I have come to see you so quickly after your visit to me." He paused: "I have found out the origin of the casket. After showing it to the Falkland Palace Curator I found out that the casket had been stolen from Falkland Palace about six months ago and that the police were informed."

Their aunt after listening to his explanation about the casket's disappearance said, "I'm not surprised," and then told him about their find of the stolen jewellery. She went on to say "Do you mind if we take the casket to the police station right away?"

Mr Reid replied, "Not at all, I would have suggested taking it there anyway. "I will take you in my car as I haven't anything to do tonight." The four of them left in his car, after Aunt Martha had locked up the cottage. He drove quite fast to the police station.

At the police station Aunt Martha handed over the casket to the constable at the desk and explained how it was found. She said that she hadn't reported the find in the first place as she hadn't known it was stolen property.

Mr Reid then told the policeman that he had seen the

curator at Falkland Palace who had confirmed that the casket had been stolen six months ago. Both Mr Reid and Aunt Martha had to write out statements about the find and these were signed and handed to the policeman.

Then Mr Reid took Aunt Martha and the children back to the cottage. Before leaving them he said, "I hope you will be all right. With the thief still at large I hope he doesn't find out where you live and that the police apprehend him soon."

Aunt Martha replied, "We will be all right – the policeman on call said he will look around this area later. That should scare the thief off from approaching us."

After hearing that a policeman would be around later Mr Reid said, "Well I'll be off. Please let me know if you are given any further information on the theft from the police." With that said he drove off quite fast to his home in Cupar. Before they went to their beds Aunt Martha made sure all the windows and doors were locked for the night.

17

The thief forces entry to the cottage

The next morning as they were eating their breakfast Aunt Martha heard loud knocking at the door. Curious who would call on her so early, yet sure that the police would have frightened off the thief, she tentatively walked to the door. She partly opened the door on the chain.

There on the step was the ugly man who had watched them in the wood when John dug up the bag of jewellery. The man put out his arm and said with a snarl, "Hand over the jewels and casket. I know you've got them."

Aunt Martha, at first taken aback, recovered her composure and said, "I haven't got the jewellery or the casket. They were handed over to the police yesterday."

The thief replied "I don't believe you. I shall be back with my mate soon so you have them ready to hand over when we return."

After the man had left Aunt Martha went into the front room and composed herself after the shock of the threat from the thief. She took the police sergeant's card off the mantelpiece and handed it to John. She instructed him, "John, if the thief returns with his accomplice, take this card with the telephone number on it and get out of the cottage without being seen and run to the telephone box and ring the policeman."

Within an hour there were thumps on the door and Aunt Martha could hear the thief shouting for her to hand over the jewellery and casket. She looked out of the window and she could see the thief with his accomplice who seemed just as menacing as the thief. She turned to John who had heard all the commotion and told him, "Get out through the back window and go through the bushes to be clear of the cottage. Once you are out of sight run down the road and ring the emergency number on the card and the operator will put you through to the police."

John with his heart in his mouth put on his jacket and climbed out the window at the back of the cottage. He crept past the side of the cottage and into the bushes. Once out of the bushes he walked quickly until he was well clear of the cottage. Then he ran down the road to the telephone box. Luckily there wasn't anyone in the box.

It took some time to get through to the local police station as the operator had several emergency calls to deal with at that time. When he did get through to the sergeant at the police station, John urgently related to him that the thief and an accomplice were at the cottage menacing his aunt at the door. He added that by now they may have forced their way into the cottage.

The sergeant, after he had heard what John had to say told him to stay by the telephone box until he picked him up, explaining to him, "It will take a little while to collect a van and enough officers to apprehend the thieves but we will be there as quickly as possible."

While John had been telephoning the police station one

of the thieves had broken a window at the front of the cottage and the two thieves had climbed into the cottage.

Although Aunt Martha and Sandra had resisted, the men overpowered them and pushed them into chairs. The ugly thief held a knife at Aunt Martha's throat and told both of them to keep still or else she will feel how sharp this was across her throat.

His accomplice looked in several cupboards and finally found an old clothes line. This he cut it up and used it to tie Aunt Martha and Sandra's hands behind their backs. Then with two scarves he gagged them by tying them around their mouths so they couldn't cry out for help.

With the accomplice watching over them, the thief started to search the cottage from top to bottom for the jewellery and the casket – looking in cupboards, pulling out drawers and after searching them throwing them on the floor. Not finding anything, the thief searched through the furniture and all over the cottage. Not finding the jewellery or the casket, the thief became very frustrated and trashed some of the ornaments in the bedrooms. The noise the thief made as the ornaments were crashing to the floor quite frightened Aunt Martha and Sandra.

As the thief was trashing the ornaments, the police van turned up at the telephone box. The sergeant stepped out of the front seat and beckoned John to jump in. Once John was in the van the policeman at the wheel drove the van slowly up to the cottage. Stopping just short of the cottage, several policemen as well as the sergeant crept up to the cottage. Seeing the broken window, two policemen carefully climbed into the cottage. At the same time the sergeant and another policeman climbed in at the back window that had been used by John to escape from the cottage.

The sergeant and policeman managed to catch the accomplice unawares and after a short struggle overpowered and handcuffed him. While one of the policemen freed Aunt Martha and Sandra, the sergeant and another constable ran up the stairs. As the thief had heard the commotion downstairs he was ready for the two policemen. Being heavy built and tall he was difficult to overpower. It took several minutes to secure the thief and pull him to the floor. Once on the floor he was forced on to his front so that he could be handcuffed with his arms behind his back.

While two of the constables were taking the thieves to the van the sergeant asked Aunt Martha and Sandra if they needed any medical attention. They both, having recovered by now from the shock of the break-in, said they were all right. Aunt Martha added that the damage was not too great with only the broken ornaments to tidy up. She turned to the sergeant and said, "We can only thank you so much for coming to our rescue so quickly. We will sleep in our beds more comfortably tonight."

The sergeant replied, "I was glad we reached you before the thieves injured anyone. You will have to visit the station and make a statement on what happened here today."

After the police had left with the thieves in the van Aunt Martha with some help from John and Sandra tidied up the rooms. Fortunately the ornaments that were smashed by the thief upstairs were not expensive items.

With the tidying-up finished the three of them sat down to a well-earned cup of tea and toast. While they were enjoying their snack Aunt Martha said John had been very brave to risk being caught by the thieves when he escaped from the cottage to call the police.

Looking at John and Sandra, she saw that they were still subdued after the frightening break in. She felt that she should do something to cheer them up so she said, "I'm sorry. You deserve a treat after your awful experience. I'll take you to Anstruther where we can visit a restaurant that is reputed to serve the best fish and chips in Fife."

John and Sandra relieved to have the frightening experience behind them readily agreed to their aunt's suggestion.

So while they were getting ready to go the aunt brought out the car. With John and Sandra comfortable in the back seat of the car she drove off from the cottage.

As it was a sunny day Aunt Martha took the cross country route across Fife. She stopped the car when they reached the village of Ceres. There she pointed out the picturesque humpback bridge nearby before driving further on the minor road to the fishing village of Pittenweem and then on along the coast road to Anstruther. At Anstruther she parked the car at the end of the harbour.

It was only a short walk from the car to the restaurant so within minutes the three of them were sitting down at one of the empty tables in the restaurant.

It didn't take long to order and their fish and chips were soon served. As it had been some time since they had their breakfast they quickly tucked into their meal.

After finishing John and Sandra seemed much more relaxed and asked their aunt if they could visit the Maritime Museum that was nearby, which she agreed to.

The visit to the museum interested John and Sandra

as there were so many exhibits to see, especially those that gave details of the old methods of working employed by the fishermen.

They were intrigued by the old photographs on display of the fishermen and their homes. How they lived was a puzzle to the children. They couldn't understand why, as some of the photographs indicated, the fishermen and their families lived upstairs in cramped spaces in their houses whereas large areas on the ground floor were used for storing nets and other fishing equipment!

When they had seen enough in the museum they walked back to the car and their aunt drove them back to Ladybank.

On going into the cottage their aunt still checked that the cottage had not been disturbed even though she knew the thieves would not return.

Aunt Martha soon had tea and sandwiches prepared which they ate in the kitchen. Afterwards they settled down in the sitting room, and talked about their trip to Anstruther. Although they didn't intend to talk about it, the conversation turned to the jewels and the break-in. To avoid them getting worried again about what had befallen them with the thieves their aunt told them, "That's enough excitement for one day. We should all go to bed early tonight." Despite their excitement at their eventful day, John and Sandra went off to their beds feeling they were now free from the menaces of scoundrels.

Their aunt took a while before she went to bed as she was still dwelling on the thieves breaking into the cottage and how either Sandra or herself could have been injured. Aunt Martha checked on John and Sandra in their rooms when she went upstairs and found they were fast asleep.

She hoped that John wouldn't have a nightmare after the trauma of the break-in.

18

A day out visiting Elie

The next day after breakfast Aunt Martha said to John and Sandra, "We will have to visit the police station today. Each one of us will have to make statements about the break-in and confrontation with the thieves."

After visiting the police station and making their statements Aunt Martha declared that they should have a day out. "We shall have a trip to Elie which you should enjoy. We won't take a picnic basket with us this time. I am going to treat you to lunch at the local inn."

Once they had returned to the car their aunt drove along the coastal route to Elie. As the weather was warm and sunny when they got there she parked the car on the area above the beach on the north side of Elie.

On leaving the car they walked along the road above the beach and climbed the bank to the old lookout tower. When they reached the tower Aunt Martha said, "The walk along the beach towards St Monance is quite pleasant."

So the three of them climbed down to the other beach and walked along the firm sand just above the sea. On their walk they could see many sea birds. Aunt Martha pointed out various breeds of gulls as well as cormorants basking in the sunshine on the rocks. The cormorants were spreading out their large wings to help them dry out after being in the water.

After they had walked about a mile along the beach they came to a rocky cliff jutting out into the beach. John stopped ahead of his aunt and Sandra and told them, "Look at the cliff – it has a thin seam of coal in the middle of it."

Aunt Martha, catching him up and looking at the cliff replied, "Yes, there is a coal seam in the cliff."

John then asked his aunt, "Do local people dig the coal out and sell it to merchants?"

She replied, "There is not enough coal there to make it profitable for commercial purposes. Besides, it would be difficult to carry the coal up from the beach and across farm land to the road."

As Aunt Martha felt they had walked far enough they turned around and walked back to the car park. From there they made their way down to the main beach that extended from the road in which the Ship Inn was situated. As they reached the bottom of the adjoining road Aunt Martha pointed out to John and Sandra what was happening on the beach.

John and Sandra couldn't believe it. There was a fully fledged cricket match taking place on the flat part of the beach not far from the Ship Inn. Both teams were dressed in white shirts and trousers. The two batsmen and wicket keeper had pads strapped on their legs just like professional teams.

The fielders were spread around the flat sand ready for catching or throwing back the ball as the bowler was just running up to bowl. On a flat area just above the beach there was a small crowd gathered as well as members of the batting side.

John and Sandra were quite amused at seeing the antics of the fielders to stop the driven ball. One fielder had to dive full length to stop the ball going into the sea. There was one particular fielder who was short and tubby who seemed to roll along to stop the ball. Yet he never let a ball pass him and he held a spectacular catch! After a while many of the fielders needed to get rid of the sand on their clothes. Some of them had smears of brown on their trousers and shirts due to their efforts when diving for balls.

Aunt Martha, John and Sandra watched the cricket for about an hour. At the end of that time John said, "I am surprised how well they play cricket on the sand."

Aunt Martha told him, "Yes, they play well considering the sand is soft. I have watched cricket matches before when I have visited Elie in previous summers." When there was a lull in the play, as one of the batsmen was bowled out, she added, "We have stayed here long enough – it's time for us to go and have our lunch."

They first went into the Ship Inn opposite the beach, but it was full of cricket enthusiasts talking about the match. From the Ship Inn they started to walk up the road leading to the main street. Looking around as they were climbing the slope, they could see the sky was getting darker. A mist had quickly came in from the sea and covered the flat area of sand. The cricket-playing area looked as if it was floating on air and the players seemed to be dancing in the mist around the wicket.

The sun came out and just as suddenly the mist rolled

back to the sea. The three of them talked about this strange illusion caused by the mist and how it changed the appearance of the players and the playing area on the beach. They continued to walk up the road until they reached the main street. There Aunt Martha pointed out a suitable restaurant where they could have a meal. On entering the restaurant they found that there were plenty of empty tables. Sitting down at one of them they ordered hamburgers and cool drinks. When their lunch was served, they soon tucked into the food as they were hungry after the walk and watching the cricket. After finishing their meal they walked around the main street window-shopping.

John and Sandra soon got tired of looking in the shop windows and asked their aunt if they could return to the cottage. Aunt Martha agreed to return as she felt tired herself after the long walk along the beach and around the village. They walked back along the main street to the turning for the road to the carpark and then after walking past the football ground reached the car park.

John and Sandra climbed into the back of the car, quite glad to sit after all the walking they had done. Their aunt drove the car away and took the direct route to Ladybank. Within minutes John and Sandra fell fast asleep and didn't wake up even when they reached the cottage. Once she had unlocked the door to the cottage she woke the children up. They couldn't believe that they had slept all the way back in the car to the cottage. That evening, after a light meal, John and Sandra were quite content to read their books for a little while and go to bed early.

19

Their last day at the end of their holiday

The next day Aunt Martha said they should have a quiet morning as their father was coming to collect them and take them back to their home in Dunfermline. It would be the end of their holiday as they would start back at their school on the following Monday.

In the afternoon their father arrived in his Morris Minor car. The car as usual was in pristine condition. Mr Brown had washed and polished it before he left Dunfermline to travel to Ladybank. On his arrival John and Sandra ran out to the car to greet him. After hugs all round he asked them if they had enjoyed their holiday.

"Very much indeed," said Sandra.

"Great," said John.

Mr Brown greeted his sister Martha and asked the three of them, "Has anything exciting happened to you during the holiday?"

"Nothing to speak of really," said Aunt Martha, then turned around and winked at John and Sandra who smiled back at their aunt's deception.

Once Mr Brown was led into the cottage and he'd sat

down, John and Sandra couldn't contain themselves any longer and had to tell him about their findings in the woods. They went on to tell him about the thieves breaking in to the cottage and how John had escaped from the cottage and telephoned the police.

"My, you have had quite an experience on your holiday. The break-in must have been worrying especially for your aunt. The main thing is that you didn't get hurt and the thieves are in custody," said their father.

After John and Sandra had finished telling their father all about the interesting places they had visited Aunt Martha sat him down to have a meal with them. When the meal was finished and the kitchen tidied up Mr Brown thanked his sister for looking after the children.

While Aunt Martha and her brother were chatting in the front room John and Sandra went upstairs and finished packing their suitcases. When they came downstairs their father put their cases in the boot of the car. Before leaving the cottage John and Sandra kissed Aunt Martha and thanked her for such an adventurous and enjoyable holiday. Aunt Martha said, "Life will be dull here when you are gone. After all that's happened, I'll be getting a telephone installed next week so you'll have to call me from time to time."

After Mr Brown repeated his thanks to his sister for looking after his children he kissed her and walked out of the cottage with John and Sandra.

With John and Sandra settled in the back seat of the Morris Minor their father prepared to drive away. John and Sandra looked out of the window and were surprised to see a young hare hop across from below a bush and stop in front of the car. It looked up at them and snuffed with its nose. Then it loped off up the road to the Lower Woods.

As their father drove them away they waved goodbye to Aunt Martha standing in the doorway of the cottage. At the end of the road Sandra turned around and looked towards the woods and said to John, "Do you think that was the young hare we befriended?"

PART TWO

FURTHER MYSTERIES OF THE LADYBANK WOODS

1

John and Sandra start their autumn holiday

As the autumn school holidays were approaching John and Sandra asked their father if they could stay with Aunt Martha again. They said their aunt had hinted that they could do so. Their father was reluctant to let them as it had been such a short time since their visit in the summer.

After some persuasion their father relented and as Aunt Martha now had a telephone installed called her that evening. Mr Brown asked his sister if she wouldn't mind John and Sandra coming to stay with her during the autumn school holiday.

He told her that initially he'd said no to their request as it had been less than two months since their visit in the summer. He felt that it would be an imposition on her.

Aunt Martha replied, "Not at all. I would love for them to visit again. We had a wonderful time together. Although I hope you won't be put out if they do visit."

Her brother replied, "Actually if they do stay with you it would suit me as I have some important business to conclude in France. And I would be able to give my housekeeper some time off as well."

"Well that settles that," said Aunt Martha.

The next week with the finish of the last lesson at school for the summer term, John and Sandra couldn't get to the school bus quick enough. On the bus all they could talk about was their forthcoming stay at Aunt Martha's home.

In their conversation they wondered if they would uncover any more secrets in the Lower Woods. Sandra, being the more down-to-earth person said, "I think it was just good fortune that you found the marked slate John."

In reply to her remark, ever the optimist, John said, "You never know what could turn up in woods that are very old."

After getting off the bus John and Sandra ran all the way home. After saying hello to the housekeeper and their father they went upstairs and completed packing their cases for the visit.

2

John and Sandra return to Ladybank

They were up early the next morning eager to be on their way to Ladybank soon after breakfast. Their father, who was always an early riser, greeted them and said jokingly, "You are up sharp this morning. I wonder why?" The three of them laughed as their father knew they normally would have lain in their beds much longer on the first day of their holiday.

Soon after breakfast Mr Brown loaded up the Morris Minor and John and Sandra quickly got into the back of the car, eager to be on their way. Their father took the coast road to Ladybank. Although a longer journey it was a more picturesque drive with views of the River Forth on the way.

As they were passing a farm near Kirkcaldy John pointed to children and adults working in a field and asked, "Dad, the children are filling baskets with potatoes lying on the ground. Why is the farmer employing children to do the work?"

In reply his father said, "Using children for this work stems from an age-old custom called 'tattie howkin'. Schools in rural areas were closed to allow children to earn money gathering potatoes for the farmer after the shaws were turned over by mechanical equipment. The work is labour intensive and back-breaking so children used in large numbers were ideal for the harvesting of the potatoes. Years ago rural families were quite poor and the money earned by the children helped to buy food to supplement the families through the winter months."

After another twenty minutes of driving Mr Brown drove into Ladybank and on to his sister's cottage. Martha Brown came out to greet them and told them how pleased she was to see them.

When they went inside the cottage she sat them down in the kitchen. When they were settled she said, "I have prepared a vegetable soup and crusty bread for you as the weather is cold for October."

When they had finished their soup Aunt Martha asked her brother if he was in a hurry to return to Dunfermline. Her brother replied, "I can stay one night as I haven't any urgent business to attend to in the office."

"Well that's good," said Aunt Martha. "You can sleep on the settee that makes up as a bed. I was happy you could stay as I have baked a cake and other savouries for my birthday tea tomorrow."

It was a quiet evening for the family. Aunt Martha brought out the game Monopoly which they played for several hours. John and Sandra were quite competitive trying to win the most hotels and stations on the board. When the game was complete their father told John and Sandra, "It's getting late – you should go to your beds now."

Once John and Sandra had gone upstairs to their rooms Aunt Martha prepared the settee bed for her brother. When this was done she said goodnight and went up to her room. James Brown soon undressed and got into the bed as he was quite tired. Within a few minutes he was fast asleep.

Upstairs Aunt Martha read her book for a while then checked on John and Sandra in their rooms and found they were sleeping soundly. Quite content she went back to her bed and was soon asleep.

In the morning James Brown walked to the shops in the main street and bought a newspaper and some groceries for his sister. Later the four of them walked to the Lower Woods. John had to show his father the hollow tree where he found the marked slate which enabled them to find the casket and stolen jewellery.

Before they walked back to the cottage Aunt Martha pointed out to the others that part of the north side of the woods had been cleared of trees.

On returning to the cottage John, Sandra and their father helped Aunt Martha prepare for the birthday tea. When the preparations were complete and the table laid, John, Sandra and their father gave their presents to Aunt Martha. These were books from John and Sandra and a gold necklace from their father.

The meal was quite delicious with so many delicacies to choose from on the table. For the sweet there was a sumptuous chocolate cake made by Aunt Martha. Once the birthday celebrations were over, James Brown said to his sister, "I am sorry but I have to leave soon as I have to make my trip tomorrow and have to be up early in the morning."

After he had packed his bag he said his farewells to John and Sandra, then he thanked his sister for looking after him for the last two days and for letting John and Sandra stay for the duration of their school holiday. With John, Sandra and Aunt Martha waving to him from the front steps, Mr Brown drove off in his Morris Minor to Dunfermline.

Returning indoors John and Sandra helped their aunt wash up in the kitchen. As it was now late in the evening John and Sandra said they were tired and went upstairs to their rooms. Aunt Martha went up to her room not long after them.

3

They visit Mrs Neil again

At breakfast Aunt Martha suggested to John and Sandra that they visit Mrs Neil in Giffordtown. The children said they would be delighted to visit her as they had enjoyed their last visit.

Aunt Martha went on to say, "I've made tentative arrangements for us to visit her. Last week, as Mrs Neil doesn't have a telephone, I put a note through her letterbox asking if we could visit her today. She called me from a telephone box the next day to say yes and added that she was looking forward to talking to you about your finds of the casket and stolen jewellery."

With the breakfast finished, Aunt Martha got out of her car and drove them to Mrs Neil's home. When they arrived, Mrs Neil welcomed them and said to John and Sandra, "Is your father staying for a few days?" Sandra replied, "No, he had to return to Dunfermline last night as he has an early start for his trip to France."

She soon had them sitting down in her front room. Without much delay she produced some tea and cream cakes for them. John and Sandra enjoyed their cream cakes so much that they were pressed by Mrs Neil to have some more. John had a great deal of the cream on his face by the time he finished his last cake.

With their tea finished, Mrs Neil asked John and Sandra about their finds – the stolen casket and jewellery in the Lower Woods. John and Sandra gave Mrs Neil an account of how they were first thwarted in their efforts to find the hiding place marked on the slate, then of their eventual success when the markings were analysed correctly. This time they had found not only the casket but the slate which led them to the hiding place of the stolen jewellery. They then related how the thieves had broken into the cottage and tied Sandra and Aunt Martha to some chairs.

Sandra told her how one of the thieves vented his anger when he couldn't find the stolen property by smashing many of the ornaments in the bedrooms. John had to show off by relating quite vividly how he escaped from the cottage to contact the police.

After John and Sandra had finished their story Mrs Neil said, "My! You have had an exciting time because of your finds in the Lower Woods. I expect you think you had unravelled all the secrets of the Lower Woods. Well, I have a surprise for you. Did you notice that quite a number of trees have been cut down at the North side of the woods?"

Aunt Martha replied, "Yes we noticed that trees had been removed when we walked through the woods yesterday."

"Well," continued Mrs Neil, "the contractors while removing the trees found two rectangular-shaped stones on which were unusual designs cut into the stones."

She went on to relate that the contractor's manager had

informed the local authorities of the find. Subsequently several officials from the council visited the site including an archaeologist.

After careful examination of the carved stones, the archaeologist declared that they were Pictish symbol stones and were over eleven hundred years old. One stone had the outline of a Pictish horsemen with shields and spears, the other had scrolls and crescent shapes carved on it. He took photographs of the stones and the surrounding area. When he had completed his inspection he told the contractor's manager that he would make arrangements for the removal of the stones so that they could be stored in a safe place. This would avoid the stones being left in the open and possibly being vandalised or stolen.

When Mrs Neil had finished explaining about the discovery of the stones Aunt Martha said, "I never thought anything like that would be found in the Lower Woods." Turning to John and Sandra she smiled: "If we visit the woods tomorrow we may be able to see the Pictish stones before they are lifted and taken away."

After chatting for a while Aunt Martha said they should return to Ladybank. She thanked Mrs Neil for her hospitality and said she would keep in touch with her.

Mrs Neil replied, "Please do come again with John and Sandra."

Aunt Martha drove back to Ladybank with John and Sandra in the back talking excitedly about the discovery of the Pictish symbol stones buried in the woods.

Long after they were back at the cottage John and Sandra still talked about the stones. They asked their aunt if she would keep to her promise and they could visit the woods the next day to see the carved stones before they were taken away.

4

A visit to the woods to see the Pictish stones

The next morning John and Sandra were up not long after their aunt who always rose early. As soon as they had their breakfast the three of them left the cottage and walked to the woods. After reaching the woods they walked along the path to the North side. As they reached the end of the woods they could see where the trees had been removed. On a closer look they could see the two carved symbol stones lying in a cleared part of the woods.

Luckily they were in time as the contractor had just arrived and the workmen were preparing to lift the stones onto a lorry. When asked by Aunt Martha, the contractor's manager gave them permission to look at the stones. They noticed that the carvings were still quite clear and showed the horsemen and other carvings well defined.

After they had looked at the stones Aunt Martha told John and Sandra that they should stand well clear of them while they were being lifted, and the manager seeing they were well clear, gave orders for the lift. His workmen tied ropes around the two stones and, using a small crane that had just arrived, lifted them onto the timbers laid on the flat back of the lorry. Then they tied down the stones onto the lorry with ropes to avoid any movement. Soon after the lorry drove away with the stones while the workmen continued clearing bushes to give them space to start cutting more trees.

Once the carved stones had been taken away Aunt Martha, John and Sandra returned to the cottage. Over morning coffee, John asked his aunt, "How did the archaeologist know the Pictish stones were over twelve hundred years old?" His aunt told him, "The archaeologist would know about their age because the Picts ceased to be a nation in the ninth century." She continued: "I will explain it simply to you.

"Kenneth MacAlpin was the early King of Scots who united the Picts and the Scots tribes in the ninth century. Kenneth inherited a kingdom that had been overcome by Scandinavian invasions and their warriors, who slaughtered many of the Picts. From this time on the Picts were absorbed in with the Scots who had moved into the East of Scotland. So the Picts were no longer prominent in this area; therefore the symbol stones would have been carved when the Picts were an important nation before 800AD."

As it was still early in the day Aunt Martha suggested that they take a trip to St Monans as there was something she wanted to show them there. They quickly prepared some sandwiches and hot soup, which they put in a vacuum flask.

5

A visit to St Monans

Within half and hour Aunt Martha was driving them to St Monans, taking the coastal path going through Lundin Links and Elie. When they reached St Monans Aunt Martha parked the car near the old church on a peninsula jutting out into the sea. From there they walked into St Monans, passing the old fishermen's cottages, and looked around the harbour.

Then they walked on through the village and on to an open stretch of shore that was mainly of rocky formation. In this area large squares were set out with low supporting walls. Just above these squares on a platform cut in the rock face a windmill was situated that had recently been restored.

When they reached the area below the windmill Aunt Martha said to John and Sandra, "This is what I wanted to show you. Years ago the windmill was used to pump salt water from the sea into the squared-off areas to form shallow pools of water. The water was left for days so that the sun gradually evaporated the water leaving the sea salt at the bottom. The local people then scraped up the salt and bagged it. This sea salt was taken away and sold to merchants for use in towns and cities for preserving meats and other perishable food."

Sandra said to her aunt, "That seems a very slow way of obtaining salt."

Aunt Martha replied, "I suppose it was a slow process, but salt years ago was quite costly to buy as it was not produced in bulk quantities the way it is obtained nowadays. At one time salt was so valuable that it was used for purchasing goods instead of money. So you see the reclaiming of this site gives an insight into our heritage."

Sandra and John said to Aunt Martha that they didn't realise that years ago salt was obtained in that way. They thought it was just dug out of the ground. She smiled. "Now you will be able to say at your school how salt was obtained years ago in Scotland."

After looking around the site and at the windmill they walked back to the car. As they were quite hungry all three of them tucked in to the sandwiches and soup. The soup was most appreciated as it was a cold day. When they had finished their meal Aunt Martha drove them back to the cottage. They quickly went into the cottage as the wind had got up and it was quite cold outside.

In the cottage after preparing and eating a cooked meal, they sat around the log fire in the front room. After the cold day they enjoyed the warmth and glow of it, insulated from the cold wind rattling the windows that evening.

6

John discovers a Bronze Age cairn

The following day John asked his aunt if they could walk to the woods and see the contractors cutting down the trees on the north side. As the wind had died down and it was warm in the sun Aunt Martha agreed to a walk in the woods. She told John, "I hope you are not expecting to find Pictish artefacts near where the carved stones were found."

"Of course not," said John, but his reply was not very convincing to either his aunt or Sandra.

So they set off well wrapped up, and headed for the woods. They took the main path to the north side and walked until they reached the area where the Pictish stones had been found. Unfortunately for John the contractors were not working in the woods that day. John, inquisitive as ever, looked around the area where the symbol stones had been uncovered, but could not find anything.

John walked towards a mound that had been partly uncovered by the removal of several trees. He walked around the top of the mound pretending to be a Pictish warrior. On the edge of the mound he slipped, displacing several large stones. Aunt Martha and Sandra had to laugh at his antics and more so when he slipped off the mound. After recovering his composure, John looked at the side of the mound where the stones had fallen away. John could see what looked like a tunnel beyond where the stones had been dislodged. He put his head into the hole and started to crawl into the tunnel until he felt something clammy on his face. As he wiped his face he realised the clamminess was caused by several spiders' webs. All of a sudden a large spider crawled along his arm, which made him jump back out of the tunnel.

John plucked up courage and entered the tunnel again. He crawled up the tunnel until it ended in a space that was circular in shape. Feeling in the dark he felt and picked up two shapes that seemed metallic. As well as these items he found a pot. With these items in his hands he gradually crawled back out of the tunnel.

Outside the mound John showed his finds to his aunt and Sandra. Looking carefully at the items John had brought out Aunt Martha said, "You have found a dagger, a brooch and a clay vessel. The dagger and brooch seem to be bronze so they must be very old. We should close up the hole to safeguard the hiding place. Then we should take the artefacts to the cottage and clean them up as they are quite dirty, with all that soil all over them."

John and Sandra couldn't get back to the cottage quick enough so that they could start cleaning the artefacts. After examining the cleaned objects Aunt Martha said, "These artefacts could be much older than the Pictish symbol stones. I will telephone my friend John Reid the historian who previously advised us on the stolen casket and ask him to visit the cottage and examine the artefacts."

That afternoon Aunt Martha telephoned Mr Reid and gave him the details of John's finds as well as the shape of the mound in the woods. When he heard all the details Mr Reid said he was very interested in examining the artefacts especially the earthenware pot. He could visit the cottage the following morning if it was convenient. Aunt Martha replied, "As we haven't planned any trips for tomorrow the morning would be fine." So a time of ten o'clock was agreed for his visit.

7

The historian visits to examine the find in the woods

The next morning Mr Reid arrived at the cottage promptly at ten o'clock. When he was shown the artefacts by John he examined them closely, taking time over each piece. When he had finished his examination he agreed with the aunt that the artefacts were very old. He went on to say, "I would like to see the mound in the woods to get more clues as to the origin of it. I have a camera and torch with me so I would like to take some photographs in the tunnel and inner chamber before it is disturbed any more."

Within minutes they were out of the cottage and into the woods, walking along the path to the mound. John showed Mr Reid where the stones were blocking the tunnel. After the stones were removed Mr Reid crawled along the tunnel, clearing cobwebs and spiders in his way.

At the end of the tunnel Mr Reid with the aid of his torch took several photographs. When he had finished he crawled back along the tunnel bringing with him another clay pot that had a different shape to the one John had found.

After brushing himself down Mr Reid replaced the stones

over the opening of the tunnel. He said, "That should avoid the mound being vandalised before I ask the official archaeologist to visit the site. I feel this is quite an important find."

On their return to the cottage Mr Reid was given a welcome cup of tea by Aunt Martha as the weather was quite cold. When he had finished his tea Mr Reid turned to John and said, "You have stumbled on an unusual find. What you have discovered is an ancient cairn, which, from examining its contents, I think dates back to the Bronze Age. This was confirmed to me when I examined the central chamber of the cairn. In the chamber I found a stone cist in which there were partly burnt remains of a human being.

"The other find I brought out was a clay pot called a bell beaker, a drinking vessel. Therefore my assessment of the age of the cairn is between 3,000 and 4,000 years old. The Beaker Folk as the tribe was called lived in this area during that period of time. These folk were known to exist in the East of Scotland from 2,400 BC onwards. Naturally I will have to get the official archaeologist to confirm my assessment of the age of the cairn and its contents."

When he had finished writing down the details of the artefacts found in the cairn he asked Aunt Martha if he could make a telephone call. Aunt Martha said that she was more than happy for him to use the telephone especially as she guessed he was going to telephone the archaeologist.

Mr Reid telephoned the archaeologist, a Mr Cameron, whom he knew well, and gave him details of the discovery of the cairn and its contents. He asked him if he could visit the site. Mr Cameron said he was free the next day and could visit the cottage in the morning at nine o'clock.

After telling the aunt and children that a visit by the archaeologist had been fixed for the next morning, Mr Reid said that he must go as he had an appointment with a customer at his office in about half an hour. He said that he would come along the next morning as he was very interested to know if his analysis of the age of the cairn and artefacts was correct.

8

The archaeologist examines the cairn and artefacts

As arranged, the archaeologist and Mr Reid called at the cottage promptly at nine o'clock the next morning. After exchanging pleasantries, Mr Reid and Mr Cameron with the aunt and children in tow walked to the woods.

Mr Reid soon had the stones removed from the mound. This allowed Mr Cameron to crawl along the tunnel and take photographs of the inner chamber. After he had crawled out and brushed himself down they all returned to the cottage.

Inside Aunt Martha made everyone a cup of tea. After they had their tea Mr Cameron confirmed the mound contained an ancient cairn. He dated it back to the Bronze Age over three thousand years ago. The clay pot further indicated that the cairn was built by the Beaker Folk who lived in this part of Scotland at this time.

He finished by saying that he would arrange for the cairn to be thoroughly examined. As much detail of the inner chamber as possible would be recorded. Any other artefacts found and the stone cist would be removed and taken to his store for safe-keeping to avoid any vandalism of the site. This would have to be done soon as once more trees were removed in the way of the mound the cairn would be exposed and easily vandalised.

Mr Cameron and Mr Reid thanked the aunt for her hospitality. Before leaving, Mr Cameron told her that he would let her know if his team found anything more around the site confirming its age and if any other artefacts were discovered. Before he left Aunt Martha handed over the artefacts that John had found.

After they had gone and for the rest of the day John and Sandra as well as Aunt Martha talked about the cairn and its artefacts. They couldn't get over being told that the cairn had existed over three thousand years ago.

Finally when the discussions on the cairn and artefacts had been exhausted, Aunt Martha said, "Let's forget about the cairn and the woods and do something completely different tomorrow. I suggest we take a trip to Dundee tomorrow and visit the famous ship *Discovery*. I feel that would be a welcome change for us."

John and Sandra agreed to the trip wholeheartedly.

They did very little for the rest of the day except for cleaning up the cottage and reading their books.

9

They visit the famous ship Discovery

When they were having their breakfast the following morning Sandra said to her aunt, "I believe the ship *Discovery* sailed to the Antarctic when Captain Scott and his team after landing trekked to the South Pole."

Her aunt replied, "That's not quite true. Scott and his team did sail on the *Discovery* to Antarctica but didn't reach the South Pole. Although they did bring back much information on the conditions and environment of that part of Antarctic that he and his team explored. It was at a later date in 1910 that Scott set out with a team to Antarctica on the ship *Terra Nova* and on landing succeeded in trekking with his team to the South Pole. With his team he reached the South Pole on 18th January 1912 to find that Amundsen a famous Norwegian explorer had preceded him by three weeks.

"Amundsen used dogs, instead of the horses used by Scott, which allowed him to make much faster trekking to the Pole. Unfortunately Scott and his main team members on their way back from the Pole to their camp were caught in a storm and died in their tent. Well that's enough explanation for now, we will learn more when we visit

Discovery," said Aunt Martha.

As soon as they had finished their breakfast they were on their way in the car to Dundee. Aunt Martha didn't prepare anything for a picnic as she said that she would treat them to a lunch in Dundee.

She took the Cupar road to Dundee and in about half an hour they were crossing the Tay River by the toll bridge at Newport. Once across the bridge Aunt Martha drove to the area where the ship *Discovery* was berthed. After the car was parked they made their way to the enclosure that contained the berth where the ship was on display.

An official guide took them and other visitors around the ship. He explained how the ship was rigged, the layout of the cabins and crew's quarters below. The guide explained how the ship had been built of very heavy timbers to withstand the severe pressure of the ice in Antarctic waters.

During their tour they could see shipwrights repairing some of the bulwarks, upper rail timbers, with adzes that had sharp bladed ends for paring the wood. Ashore in one of the nearby buildings workmen were repairing masts and splicing ropes for use on the rigging of the ship.

The guide then told them about Scott's voyage to Antarctica on board *Discovery* in detail. At the end of the tour Aunt Martha thanked the guide for his most informative tour of the ship. Leaving the enclosure the three of them made their way to the car.

Aunt Martha drove the car into the centre of Dundee and parked the car. As they were quite hungry Aunt Martha lost no time in taking John and Sandra to her favourite restaurant for lunch. After lunch the three of them wandered around the shops. Aunt Martha bought some Christmas presents for friends and her brother. John and Sandra bought Christmas presents for their father and housekeeper.

With all their packages they returned to the car quite content with their purchases. Aunt Martha took a different route back to Ladybank. She chose a more rural route passing a number of woods where the trees showed up their autumn colours. The fading leaves displaying a mixture of brown, yellow and red colours. Sandra remarked, seeing the sunshine through one of the trees, "It looks as if the tree is on fire.

When they reached the cottage they went in and after a cup of tea started to prepare a meal for the evening. After their meal John and Sandra were happy to have a quiet evening.

10

Bad news when they return to the cottage

After only being in the cottage for about half an hour Aunt Martha had a telephone call. When she came back into the kitchen she was quite pale and upset. Sandra asked her aunt, "What is troubling you?" She explained to Sandra and John that the telephone call was from the police. The sergeant at the station had informed her that the thief, who had hidden the jewellery in the woods, had escaped and was possibly hiding in the Lower Woods near the cottage. The policeman added that one of his constables would be keeping a watch in the vicinity of the woods for the thief.

Despite this reassurance by the sergeant Aunt Martha said after their meal, "We better make sure all the windows and doors are locked this evening." So after a quiet evening by the log fire they all went to bed early. John and Sandra were soon asleep, but Aunt Martha read in bed as she couldn't sleep for thinking about the thief who may have been hiding in the nearby woods and possibly thinking about some means of revenge on her. At last she managed to sleep and fortunately the cottage was not disturbed that night.

At breakfast John said he had a terrible dream. He dreamt that the thief had come out of the woods and crept up to the cottage, climbed up a drainpipe, then rattled on the windows. This was too much for John and he woke up with a start. He was much relieved that it was only a dream as he was still worried that the thief may be hiding nearby in the woods.

Later in the morning Aunt Martha had a telephone call from the police station. The sergeant told her that the thief had been apprehended in the woods and was now back in prison.

When Aunt Martha told John and Sandra that the thief had been caught she could see the relief on their faces. Relieved herself, Aunt Martha said, "I just have to buy some food in the local shops in Ladybank. With the thief still being at large I didn't want to risk our having to go out of the cottage. Then for the rest of the day we will have a quiet day at home." After all the worry and excitement this suited John and Sandra.

11

The three celebrate Halloween

After a quiet morning at the cottage Aunt Martha proposed that they should celebrate Halloween. This was wholeheartedly agreed to by John and Sandra as they had been to Halloween parties before in Dunfermline.

Aunt Martha suggested that they dress up in costumes to celebrate Halloween and make up a play and perform it to Mrs Neil as they had been invited to visit her at her home in Charlottown.

John was dressed up to look like a ghost with a white sheet and his face whitened with flour. Sandra was dressed up as a witch with a black dress and a peaked hat made up by her aunt. For herself Aunt Martha dressed up as a kitchen maid with her head topped with a long black-haired wig. They were all in fits of laughter seeing each other in their costumes. Aunt Martha explained the play she had made up to them.

They performed the play a couple of times to get used to the parts they had to play. Early in the evening Aunt Martha drove them over to Mrs Neil's home in Charlottown. After knocking at her door there was a short delay before Mrs Neil opened it. She roared with laughter seeing them in their costumes.

They were welcomed into the house, but she said to them, "Before you get some tea and cream cakes I must see you perform your play that your aunt told me she had composed. As they had rehearsed their parts earlier the three of them quite readily gave their performance of the little play.

John as the ghost had to appear and make weird noises and then be driven off by Aunt Martha as the maid. Then Sandra as the witch appeared and tried to put a spell on the maid but the maid forestalled her and drove her out of the room with a broom.

When they had finished the play Mrs Neil clapped her hands in glee, having enjoyed their antics during the performance of the play. "Excellent, you all played your parts well," said Mrs Neil. "Now you deserve to have your tea and cream buns."

When they had finished their tea and buns, Mrs Neil wanted to know about their further finds in the woods. Aunt Martha related how, after they had seen the Pictish stones being taken away, John stumbled on the entrance to a cairn. She went on to tell how they had a visit by the historian and then by him and the official archaeologist. She went on to explain that the archaeologist after his examination of the cairn confirmed that it was over three thousand years old. He and his team took away many artefacts including the stone cist for safekeeping in his store.

After Aunt Martha had finished Mrs Neil said, "My! You did have an exciting find, John. Sandra and yourself will have much to tell your father and school friends."

As they had been at Mrs Neil's home some time Aunt Martha felt that they should return to the cottage. She thanked Mrs Neil for her hospitality.

"Not at all," said Mrs Neil. "Your visits here I look forward to, especially when you relate so many exciting stories of mysterious finds in the woods."

Soon after, the three of them left the house, Mrs Neil as usual waving to them on her front steps as Aunt Martha drove back to the cottage.

On their return John and Sandra helped Aunt Martha to prepare a light meal. After their meal Aunt Martha said, "As it's Halloween we should finish off the evening with some traditional games." She got out a tin bath from a cupboard and filled it with water and then dropped into the water a bucket of apples. "Now we will duck for apples; you can go first, John." John in his usual boisterous way said, "This will be easy for me."

Once he started to duck into the water for an apple he didn't find it so easy. Every time he ducked into the water the apples bobbed away from him. After many goes he took it more slowly and managed to catch an apple in his teeth and lift it out of the bath – except the front of his jumper was soaked with water and had to be taken off. Sandra and Aunt Martha were much more careful and caught apples in their teeth without getting too wet.

In the next game, Aunt Martha set up strings with buns attached covered in treacle. This time they had to kneel on a chair with its back facing the buns. Each one of them had to bite the buns with their arms behind their backs. Again, John was in too much of a hurry and ended up with treacle all over his face. In their turns Sandra and her aunt were much more careful and took bites out of the buns without much treacle on their faces.

For the final game, Aunt Martha pinning a drawing of a donkey on a board that had a tail missing. She had made up a donkey's tail from a piece of cardboard to use in the game. She explained to Sandra and John that there was a pin through the tail so that it could be pinned onto the figure of the donkey. She went on to say that each one of them would be blindfolded in turn then they would be spun around several times and then be given the tail to pin on the drawing of the donkey. She emphasised that the one closest to pinning the tail in the right place would be the winner.

When Sandra was blindfolded and spun around she was quite dizzy and pinned the tail on the front end of the donkey. This caused much laughter from John and Aunt Martha. Aunt Martha was a little better as the spinning didn't make her so dizzy and she ended up pinning the tail on the donkey's stomach! John was the most successful and after he was blindfolded and spun around he didn't feel dizzy. He ended up pinning the tail on the back end of the donkey. He whooped for joy when he took off his blindfold and found out how successful he had been with the pinning of the tail.

With the games finished, Aunt Martha prepared hot drinks for everyone. Once they'd had their drinks, John and Sandra were quite happy to go to their beds after such an exciting and enjoyable day.

12

Sandra and John become ill

During the night Aunt Martha was awake with the sounds of John and Sandra's bouts of coughs and sneezes. She wondered if they had caught colds, as during the day she noticed that their faces were quite flushed when they were playing games. As the games were quite active she didn't take too much notice at the time.

As she lay awake she could hear the wind rattling the slates on the roof, becoming stronger and stronger. Before she fell asleep the wind had increased to storm level. She could hear the wind roaring through the trees in the nearby woods.

The next morning after rising later for once, after a disturbed sleep, Aunt Martha was surprised that John and Sandra hadn't come down from their rooms. She left them for half an hour and then went up to see them and tell them how late in the morning it was and they should get up now.

When she went into Sandra's room Aunt Martha was surprised that Sandra was still in her bed. Right away Aunt Martha could see that Sandra was very ill, gasping for breath and feverish. On going into John's room she found him to be in the same feverish state as his sister.

Right away she went downstairs and brought up hot drinks for them which seemed to soothe them a little. With the drinks Aunt Martha brought up a thermometer. On checking each one of their temperatures she found that both Sandra and John had very high temperatures. When asked by Aunt Martha how they felt both said they had pains in their chest and their coughing made them gasp for breath.

With quite a worried look Aunt Martha said to John and Sandra that what they had was much more serious than a cold with their high temperatures and fever. "I am going to telephone for a doctor to come out to see you as you are not well enough to go outside in the cold and stormy weather," she said.

With that said she went downstairs and telephoned the local doctor. When the doctor rung her back she explained the symptoms of their illness to him. He agreed with her that their illness was much more serious than a cold. The doctor added that as soon as he had finished seeing the patients in his waiting room he would drive out afterwards and examine the children.

In the meantime Aunt Martha filled up hot water bottles and put them in John and Sandra's beds. To give them extra warmth, she put another blanket on each of their beds as the rooms were quite cold as a result of the stormy weather. She fetched extra pillows to help raise each one of them up in their beds to relieve the congestion on their chests that they were troubled with while lying down.

An hour later the doctor's car drew up outside the cottage and he came in and greeted Aunt Martha, as he knew her as one of his patients. He went upstairs and thoroughly examined Sandra and John and commented on their feverishness and high temperature to Aunt Martha. Turning to her he said, "I am sorry to say the children are quite ill as they have influenza and should be kept in bed for several days at least. You should give them plenty of hot drinks to help clear their chest infection. I will give you a prescription for antibiotics for them to take for the next seven days. I am glad they have been caught early for if they had gone out in this stormy weather they could have ended up with pneumonia which would have been much more serious for them."

When he had finished giving Aunt Martha instructions for the children's care she said, "There is a problem – the children are due back at school next Monday."

The doctor replied "That's not possible as even if they recover quickly they shouldn't go out in this cold and stormy weather until they have completed their courses of antibiotics. As I said earlier if they get a chill in this cold weather their illness could develop into pneumonia."

"Well that settles that problem," said Aunt Martha. "I shall telephone their father tonight when he returns from his business visits. The children can stay here until they are fully recovered."

The doctor thought for a moment: "I know you will look after them well, Miss Brown, but it could be at least two weeks before they are fully recovered. I shall call in tomorrow morning to examine the children again. It will take a few days before we see the effects of the antibiotics and the rest in bed. Let me know right away if the children become any worse."

Aunt Martha said, "Yes, I will if they get worse, but I

see a little improvement already with their being propped up in warm beds and taking their hot drinks."

After he had handed over the prescription to Aunt Martha the doctor left the cottage and drove off in his car. Aunt Martha came back to Sandra and John and like a broody hen had to tuck them in and prop them up better in their beds. Later, after returning from the chemist, Aunt Martha made sure the children took their antibiotics and more hot drinks.

Early in the evening she gave them some warm vegetable soup, which was the only sustenance that they had had all day. They had refused anything before as their throats were so sore with the endless coughs and sneezes. When they had finished their soup John and Sandra said they were quite tired and would try to get to sleep. Aunt Martha, seeing they were exhausted with the coughing and previous lack of sleep, left them, putting the lights out as she left their rooms.

13

Their father is told of the children's serious illness

That evening Aunt Martha telephoned her brother and told him that John and Sandra had influenza. She went on to say that she had called in her doctor and he had prescribed antibiotics for them. She went on to explain that the doctor had told her that the children would have to stay indoors for a week. Then they would need another week to recuperate.

Their father, recovering from the shock of hearing of his two children's illness, thanked his sister for calling in her doctor. He said, "I hope you don't mind looking after John and Sandra for all that time."

Aunt Martha replied, "Of course I don't mind. I wouldn't think of them going anywhere else to recover from their illness. Anyway the weather is too bad for them to travel."

To finish, Mr Brown said, "I shall telephone the children's schools on Monday and explain about their absence being due to illness. Thank you for looking after John and Sandra. I shall come and visit them tomorrow evening after I have cleared my business for the day."

After telephoning her brother, Aunt Martha sat in the

front room and for the first time that day relaxed. She made herself a cup of tea and then went to her bed. It was quite a worrying night for her as in her own bed she could hear John and Sandra coughing on several occasions. Later that night when Aunt Martha looked in the children's rooms she could see they were sleeping peacefully.

14

John and Sandra start to recover

The next morning when Aunt Martha brought up hot drinks for John and Sandra she could see some improvement in their condition. They didn't cough as much and the tightness of their chests seemed to have eased.

Later that morning the doctor visited the cottage and examined Sandra and John. After his examination of the children he told Aunt Martha that they were making good progress, but had a long way to go before they were out of danger of the influenza developing into something more serious. Before leaving, the doctor told Aunt Martha that he would come back in two days unless she telephoned that the children's illness was getting worse.

In the afternoon John and Sandra's father arrived. After the strain of looking after the children Aunt Martha was pleased to see her brother. Their father brought with him lots of fruit and some chocolates. He was pleased with the news from his sister that John and Sandra were over the worst of their illness.

He stayed for several hours chatting to Sandra and John. Before he left he said to his sister that he would telephone her the next evening to see how they were faring. That night Sandra and John didn't cough so much and their feverishness had lessened.

Feeling that the children had got over the worst of their illness Aunt Martha felt more confident about their recovery. For the first time that week she slept well.

When the doctor visited the cottage on the Thursday and examined the children he found them much better. When he told Aunt Martha that he was pleased with their progress she was much relieved. He did add that only if they felt better could they come downstairs at the end of the week. By the end of the week Sandra and John were over the worst of their illness. Their temperatures were back to normal and their coughing bouts had eased.

15

Ladybank experiences a storm with severe winds

The progress of the children's recovery from influenza was mirrored in the gradual abatement of the storm and its daily effect on two young trees at the edge of the wood that was visible from Sandra and John's bedroom windows. On the first day of the storm when it was at its height Sandra and John were at the worst state of their illness. The wind roared through the trees in the wood and hitting the two young trees bending them to near breaking point. The leaves were ripping off the two young trees and swirling around their slender trunks as if signalling their demise.

On the second day as Sandra and John's illness eased so did the storm. The wind still rushed through the trees in the wood but the two young trees resisted the force of the wind. More leaves came off the young trees but they swirled around on the lower parts of the slender trunks of the trees.

By the third and fourth days Sandra and John showed signs of recovery from their illness, which again was mirrored with the easing of the wind and the two young trees standing tall and straight against the lessening wind.

Despite the storm there were still leaves left on the trees. This gave Sandra much relief as she felt that their recovery from illness was linked to the withstanding of the two trees against the storm.

16

Sandra and John at last come downstairs

With the continued recovery of Sandra and John from their illness Aunt Martha allowed them to come downstairs on the Saturday. When she saw them up for the first time she was surprised to see how thin they looked. She cooked them a beef stew which they found most appetising and filling. Realising how hungry they were, they tucked into the meal and then asked for more.

After their meal they sat in the front room and the three of them played their favourite game Monopoly. Later in the evening after they had been given hot drinks John and Sandra were quite happy to go to their beds.

On the Sunday after breakfast Aunt Martha encouraged Sandra and John to take a short walk to the woods as the weather was now quite calm and warm. Sandra and John enjoyed the walk as they hadn't enjoyed being cooped up indoors all week.

The gradual easing of their illness was again mirrored with the two young trees at the edge of the wood standing straight and unbroken.

17

They visit an old cottage

The following day Aunt Martha suggested that a longer walk in the mild air would do Sandra and John some good and help them get back to a fit state for their return to school.

She told them that she was going to show them something of interest. "It's an old cottage I am looking after for an old couple who are staying in Glenrothes with their son for about a month. The husband of the couple had a hip replacement recently and needs care during his convalescence. You will find the interior of the cottage unusual as it has changed little in a hundred years. The husband's father and grandfather were born and brought up in the cottage. Not one of them changed the décor or furniture in their lifetimes there."

Sandra and John readily agreed to the walk and the three of them were soon on their way to the old cottage, which was about a mile away from Aunt Martha's home. When they reached the old cottage John asked his aunt about the large stone that was partly sunk in the ground at the corner of the cottage. Aunt Martha explained to John that the stone was called a 'dunt stane'. It was placed there to prevent cart wheels from hitting and damaging the adjoining fence when a cart was turning into the road at the side of the cottage.

Entering the cottage John and Sandra noticed that the walls didn't have any wallpaper on them, they only had a whitewash coating on them. The cottage didn't have any electric lights; each room had gas lamps with gauzes instead of lamps to give out the light.

The front room had a dark wood floor with some loose carpets. In front of the fireplace was a small settee with cloths covering two chairs, one was a rocking chair and the other a simple wooden chair with a straight back. The lack of furniture made the room look quite stark although the settee and chairs had cushions on them. When she sat in the rocking chair Sandra found it quite comfortable. The large open fireplace was set in the wall with a wrought iron grate and a large hook suspended above it. Aunt Martha explained when asked that the hook was used to hang large hams which would be preserved by smoke from the fire.

In front of the fireplace was a tiled area with a brass fender. There was a fireguard in front of the fireplace to stop hot coals falling onto the wooden floor. The only other furniture in the room was a sideboard with some small ornaments on its top.

In the kitchen there was a heavy wooden table with four upright backed wood chairs. On the long wall set in the stonework was a cooking range. The range was made up with a fire grate on the right hand side with the flat hob above it – in the hob two removable circular wrought iron plates. Aunt Martha explained that these plates could be removed so that pans of water could be placed over the openings above the fire so that the water could be boiled. When the plates were set back flush into the hob the top could be used for simmering any pans of soup or water on the hob.

Again there was a tiled area between the cooking range and the wooden floor. On the wall at the side of the range were secured shelves on which sat numerous jars that contained spices and other ingredients for use in preparing meals.

Opposite the range against the wall was a freestanding dresser. This was stocked with crockery and other kitchen items. It looked as if the kitchen was used much more than the front room.

The only other item in the room was a large tin bath hanging on the wall next to the dresser. Again Aunt Martha explained that this was used by the couple for bathing as the cottage didn't have a bathroom.

Aunt Martha went on to explain that the only improvement that the couple had undertaken in the cottage was for a plumber to fit a toilet and washbasin in a large walk-in cupboard. She added that this had only been done in the last three or four years because the couple were getting older and going to the outside toilet in winter did cause them to catch chills or colds.

In the single bedroom again the room was quite stark containing only a single wardrobe, two wooden chairs as well as a double bed with a small carpet next to it. The only ornaments were two vases set side by side on the windowsill.

Aunt Martha went on to explain that originally the

cottage did have a single bed in the kitchen but as it hadn't been used for years the recess that the bed had been in had been boarded up years ago.

After wandering around the inside of the cottage after opening all the windows to let some fresh air in the three of them went out the back door into the garden. There Aunt Martha opened the door to the lean-to building and showed John and Sandra the layout of the inside.

In one corner there was a copper boiler with a fire grate under it. She explained that this was the main means of washing clothes. Then she showed them the heavy mangle, operated by hand, freestanding, next to the boiler, that the couple used for squeezing water out of the heavy blankets used on the bed.

On the wall opposite the boiler under the window was a deep earthenware trough used for washing the soap out of the boiled clothes. Next to the basin was a flat top of wood which was grooved to let the water run off from the washed clothes. Perched on the wooden top was a scrubbing board for getting the worst of dirt off the clothes before being put in the boiler.

Aunt Martha went on to say that the task of cleaning blankets and other heavy clothes was quite an arduous task and took up quite a good part of a day to accomplish. She went on to explain that it was a habit with the old couple to always do their heaving washing on a Monday. It was mainly done by the wife although her husband did the mangling work. When they were finished they were quite tired with the physical effort needed to tend to cleaning, boiling and mangling of the heavy clothes.

In the lean-to building on the other side of the wall

from the wash house was the outside toilet. It was still in use and quite clean. On the side wall instead of a toilet roll there was hung on a nail pieces of an old newspaper cut up neatly into squares and rectangles. Sandra pointed out the pieces of newspaper, saying laughingly to her aunt, "I can't imagine people using pieces of newspaper in a toilet."

Aunt Martha replied, "Oh yes, it was common practice to use old newspapers as people were very thrifty years ago especially when they had poor wages. Toilet paper would be considered a luxury and an old newspaper wouldn't cost anything if it was picked up after it had been read and discarded."

18

Sandra discovers a hidden box

The three of them went back into the cottage. Immediately Aunt Martha started to brush the dust up in the rooms. While she was working Sandra and John out of curiosity looked in the cupboards. In one of the cupboards Sandra and John found some of the old couple's clothes. John put on a tweed jacket which reaches down to his knees. Sandra put on an apron and lifts a cap off one of the hooks. She asked her aunt what the cap was used for indoors. Her aunt replied, "It endearingly was called a grannie mutch cap. It was used by older women indoors to protect their hair. It was very practical when women were doing dirty work indoors."

With the clothes on Sandra and John paraded around the rooms pretending they were back in the Victorian times even putting pots on and off the cooking range. While at their play Sandra walked to a corner of the kitchen. All of a sudden a floor plank she was standing on cracked and the end of the plank on which she was standing dropped below the level of the floor. Sandra lifted the broken piece of plank hoping to replace it. Just as she was replacing the piece she saw a wooden box in the hole below the opening.

Sandra tried to lift out the wooden box, but found it was too heavy and awkward for her to lift out. She shouted to her aunt and John who were in the front room. John had wandered off before Sandra found the box. Aunt Martha and John came into the kitchen wondering why she had shouted for them. Sandra lifted out the broken piece of plank so that they could see the box. Aunt Martha and Sandra between them, after some manoeuvring, managed to lift out the box. As they were lifting out the box they could hear the chink of coins.

When the box, which Aunt Martha said was made of oak, was placed on the floor clear of the hole Sandra lifted the hasps securing the lid. With the lid back on its hinges the three of them looked in the box. On top of what looked like a leather bag was two letters and a package. Sandra lifted these out and put them beside the box. Then she opened the bag by undoing its drawstring closure.

She stood back in amazement as shining in the light were a large amount of unusual gold-coloured coins. Aunt Martha picked out a few of the coins and examined them carefully. "What coins are they?" asked Sandra.

Her aunt replied, "They are gold sovereigns and are over one hundred years old. These were equal to one pound in value before paper money replaced them. Judging by their age they will be worth many times their original value. It seems strange how they may have been hidden there for maybe over a hundred years."

After recovering from the surprise of so valuable a find Aunt Martha said, "We must go back for the car as the box with the coins in it is so heavy. We should get these coins into safekeeping as quickly as possible."

19

Further revelations about their find

Before they left the cottage Aunt Martha, with John's help, moved the box to a corner where it couldn't be seen by any prying eyes at the window. After Aunt Martha locked the door of the cottage the three of them started to walk back to Aunt Martha's home.

On their way back to the cottage they were buzzed by two young lads on a motor cycle. They were cat-calling Aunt Martha as they passed them on their noisy machine. John wanted to have a go at them, but his aunt told him, "Ignore them as they won't harm us."

Without any more trouble they reached the cottage. Aunt Martha fetched her keys for the car and drove them back to the old couple's cottage. In the cottage Aunt Martha and John manhandled the heavy box out of the cottage and placed it in the boot of the car. As soon as she had locked up the cottage she drove them back to her home.

Again it needed two of them to lift the box out of the boot and take it into the cottage. With the box safely placed in the kitchen, Aunt Martha lifted out the letters and package and put them beside the box. She lifted the bag of coins onto the table and counted them. At the same time she checked the dates of their being minted. Her count showed them that there had been fifty-two sovereigns in the bag. Aunt Martha told Sandra and John all these coins could be worth well over five hundred pounds.

Next Aunt Martha looked at the two letters and package that had been in the box. The first letter she looked at was an official one that was dated May 1840. This was quoting the sale of a farm for £100 for Mr Clark, the ancestor of the husband of the old couple. The package gave details of the equipment sold with the farm.

The other letter was in the form of a note from Mr Clark's cousin dated June 1840. In his note he thanked Mr Clark for paying a large sum for his passage to Canada. He said he would be meeting up with the family of a distant cousin who had emigrated to Nova Scotia after being forced off his croft during one period of the clearances in the Scottish Highlands.

Just as Aunt Martha was putting the coins, package and letters back in the box Sandra stopped her. "Wait, Aunt Martha, look at the stamps on the official package and letter. I think the stamps are a Victorian penny black and a twopenny blue one. I saw these stamps described in a book about stamps belonging to a friend who collects them."

Aunt Martha for the first time looked properly at the stamps: "You're right, Sandra I never took any notice of the stamps what with concentrating on checking the sovereigns in the bag. I now notice that the one penny black is stamped or marked. On the package the mark has missed the twopenny blue stamp."

Aunt Martha took another look inside the official

package and letter. Inside the package was a large folded envelope with an unmarked twopenny blue stamp. In the other official letter was an envelope with an unmarked penny black stamp. Aunt Martha remarked that the official letter had asked for a reply. Similarly, the package with the details of the farm machinery attached also were supposed to be returned to the solicitor.

"Maybe Mr Clark instead of returning the documentation went to the solicitor and confirmed the sale, therefore not needing to reply to the letter or return the details in the package," said Aunt Martha. "We thought the sovereigns were valuable, but these stamps could be valued at even more. At a guess they could be worth more than a thousand pounds. It is now even more urgent that I contact Mr Clark's son in Glenrothes and ask him to come here soon so that the box can be put in a safe place."

Once the coins and letters were put back in the box Aunt Martha with John's help carried it to a small cupboard in the front room and placed it on the bottom shelf and locked up the cupboard. Tempting though it was to leave it under the floorboard where it had lain undisturbed for all this time, now the floorboard was so obviously broken it really wasn't quite so safe any longer. With that done, Aunt Martha sighed with relief that the box was safe from prying eyes. Thinking about the valuables being in the cottage brought back memories of the time when the thief broke into the cottage demanding back the stolen jewellery they had found in the woods.

20

Mr Clark's son collects the box

That evening Aunt Martha telephoned Mr Clark's son Roy at his home in Glenrothes. She gave him full details of how the box of coins, package and letters had been found in his parents' old cottage. After explaining the find, she told him she was anxious that the box should be kept in a safe place because of the value of its contents.

Roy Clark replied, "Yes, of course. I'll drive over to your cottage in about an hour's time."

So later that evening Roy Clark who she knew well through her association with his parents arrived at the cottage. He was welcomed in by Aunt Martha and introduced to Sandra and John. Once he was settled, with John's help, she removed the heavy box from the cupboard and set it before Roy Clark. Although he was told what the contents were in the box he was amazed when he saw so many sovereigns. After looking at the letters and package he agreed with her that the stamps were Victorian one penny blacks and twopenny blues.

He smiled: "This is an amazing find. If you hadn't found the box it could have lain hidden for many more years without being found. It is like turning the clock back to the year 1840. My father told me about his grandfather selling his farm but what happened to the money was a mystery. The grandfather was very secretive and he kept his business dealings to himself. A couple of years after he sold the farm he died suddenly and the family never knew what had happened to the residue of the money from the sale of the farm. I had plans to modernise the old cottage and put in an electricity system and a new bathroom, but I didn't have the funds for it after modernising my own house."

Turning to Aunt Martha and children he said, "Thank you for taking all the trouble over rescuing the box. I have a friend in Edinburgh who is a collector of rare coins and stamps. I should be able to take the box over to him tomorrow. I will let you know if the coins and stamps are as valuable as you suggested on the telephone." Without any more delay Roy Clark took the box to the car and drove back to Glenrothes.

Once he had gone, Aunt Martha said, "Now that is an end to all the excitement – we shall have a quiet evening." During the rest of the evening even though Aunt Martha told them not to bring up the subject of the items in the box Sandra and John couldn't help talking about the find and what the contents of the box were worth.

Just before Sandra and John were going to their beds Sandra told to her aunt, "I am sorry I didn't tell you before what with all the excitement over the find of the box, but I left my scarf at the old cottage. Do you mean to return there soon? If so I'd like to collect it."

Aunt Martha replied, "Yes, I intended to return to the old cottage as I would like to look under the floor where we found the box to see if there is anything else that's been hidden there over the years. So how about we visit the old cottage tomorrow and we can collect your scarf?"

Even though Sandra and John went up to their beds they were still talking about finding the coins and stamps through the open doors. After quite a while Aunt Martha felt they had chatted long enough and shouted up to them, "Go to sleep it's very late."

When Aunt Martha went upstairs later Sandra and John were fast asleep.

21

They revisit the old cottage

The next day after breakfast Aunt Martha said, "As I promised yesterday we'll visit the old cottage and collect your scarf, Sandra."

As the weather was cold and windy the three put on heavy coats before they left. As they were walking down the country road towards the old cottage they could see the two Craig brothers at the end of a side road, not far from their father's smallholding. One brother was building a bonfire with tree offcuts, leaves and rubbish. The other brother was taking pot shots at rabbits with an airgun.

Walking on, they reached the old cottage and went in. Sandra searched and found her scarf while Aunt Martha lifted the broken piece of floor plank in the kitchen. Ever curious, Sandra and John came over and watched Aunt Martha search under the floor with her hands for anything else hidden close to where the box was found. To Sandra and John's disappointment all she found was a couple of ancient flint tools. Aunt Martha raised herself up and said, "I'm sorry that's all I could find under the floor. I shall pass the flints on to my friend the historian, he would like to have them."

After replacing the broken plank Aunt Martha checked out the rest of the cottage to make sure the back door and windows were secure. This done she locked up the main door and the three of them started to walk back along the country road.

As they reached the adjoining road they could see the Craig brothers trying to light the bonfire. It was smoking without any flames. They could see one of the brothers pouring what looked like petrol from a can on the bonfire. There was a woosh as the petrol caught on fire and the bonfire became a blaze of flame.

With the strong wind, sparks and lighted paper were soon blown into the undergrowth nearby. Quite quickly the edge of the woods was on fire. The brothers tried to beat out the fire in the woods with spades but their efforts were futile as the fire crept into the woods like fuses on gunpowder kegs.

Aunt Martha and the children watching the antics of the Craig brothers were transfixed for a minute or so. Aunt Martha, realising the danger of the woods being on fire and the Craig's house being nearby, took the situation in hand. She gave the keys of her cottage to John, who could run fast and said, "Go and telephone for the fire brigade before the fire in the woods gets out of hand."

John started to run along the road to the cottage. One of the Craig brothers seeing him running picked up his airgun and fired it at him. John, as he was running, felt a burning sensation on his face. When he felt his cheek there was blood running down it.

He soon reached the cottage and once inside telephoned for the fire brigade. Still feeling the blood running down his cheek, he staunched it with a handkerchief until his aunt and Sandra arrived. After he had told his aunt that he had got a call in for the fire brigade, Aunt Martha cleaned the wound on his cheek and put a plaster over the cut.

By this time the fire brigade had arrived in the area and was tackling the part of the woods that was on fire. After about an hour of dowsing the fire with water the fire was put out. Only the upper part of the woods was still smouldering and the firemen were dowsing this area with water.

At the cottage Aunt Martha decided to take John to the doctor's surgery to have the wound to his cheek examined. After driving to the surgery she managed to get an appointment for John. The doctor examined the wound on John's cheek and put on a dressing with tapes. He told Aunt Martha that there wasn't any damage to the eye but gave her several dressings to take away and use until the wound had healed.

On their return to the cottage John strutted around the rooms saying, "I'm a war hero." After a while, Sandra, who was washing dishes in the kitchen, got fed up with his antics and threw a wet dishcloth at him. She got a direct hit on his neck. After he had dried himself off with a towel he was much more subdued.

Later that day the local policeman visited and took down the details of the cause of the fire and the wound on John's face.

Soon after settling down for the evening in the front room there was a knock at the door. Aunt Martha went and opened it. There on the doorstep was Mr Craig, the father of the two brothers. As she knew him as he had done odd jobs for her in the cottage, she invited him in. After he had sat down he said, "I must apologise for what my sons have done, especially Jim who shot your nephew with his airgun. I have destroyed the airgun and banned both of them from using the motorcycle for a month. For further punishment they have to dig over the ground set aside for growing vegetables next year."

When he had finished Aunt Martha had to tell him that the police had visited and taken statements from them. After again expressing his apologies for what his sons had done, Mr Craig left the cottage.

"Well," said Aunt Martha, "Mr Craig's punishment will teach the two sons a lesson. Although I don't think they have been in trouble before. They were just foolish putting petrol on the bonfire. After all the excitement I think we should spend the rest of the evening quietly in the front room catching up on our reading."

Despite the fire and John getting wounded, the three of them slept well that night.

22

They examine the damage to the woods

The next day out of curiosity they took a walk down the road to where part of the woods had been destroyed by the fire. When they reached the spot they could see that the fire had destroyed quite a large area. When they felt the ground it was still warm.

John, ever curious, had to explore further into the woods to see if he could find any artefacts. But soon he found his feet were sinking beneath him and his shoes were becoming difficult to lift out of the mud.

Before he had walked any further, someone shouted at him to stop. A man came up to him and said, "I'm the local forester; you shouldn't go into the woods any further – it's very boggy in there."

John said, "I didn't think the ground was too bad to walk on."

The forester replied, "That's the danger with the bog here. I'll show you how bad it is in there," pointing to the bog. He picked up a heavy stone and threw it into the middle of it. There was a sucking noise and the stone completely disappeared.

The forester led John back along a well-trodden path

back to John's aunt and Sandra. As they came out of the woods the forester explained to them the danger of the bog. Aunt Martha scolded John and said, "Trust you to go exploring without checking the place was safe." Thanking the forester, she led John and Sandra away from the burnt area of the woods.

"Now we'll do something less dangerous. We'll go for a walk in the woods near the cottage." So John and Sandra were quite happy to continue the walk to the other woods they knew were quite safe.

Beyond the cottage they reached the Lower Woods and walked along the path. They continued their walk past the hollow tree and on to the clearing at the north end where they sat in the grass for a while.

On the way back they went off the path to the high bank. There they were lucky to see two hares, one larger than the other, who had come out of their nest with the spell of warm weather. The hares scampered away when they saw Aunt Martha and the children.

The three of them continued their walk back to the cottage where they had a cup of tea.

22

They visit Mrs Neil again

That evening, Aunt Martha said to Sandra and John, "We should visit Mrs Neil again, as it's only a couple of days before your father comes to pick you up and take you back to Dunfermline. If you agree, I will telephone her tonight and confirm that we can visit her tomorrow. She did express a wish to see you before your return."

The next morning their aunt drove them to Mrs Neil's home. When they arrived the old lady was pleased to see them and soon had them sitting down comfortably in her front room.

"Well," she said, "what's been happening to you lately?"

Sandra was first to speak. "I accidentally discovered a hidden treasure below the floor in the old cottage that Aunt Martha is looking after for the Clark family." Aunt Martha helped to fill in on Sandra's account, explaining how Sandra had stood on a floorboard that collapsed as a result of dry rot. "While trying to put it back she found a heavy oak box underneath the floor. To our surprise we found fifty-two golden sovereigns in the box that had dates on them in the 1830s. On top of the bag of coins were letters which at first we didn't take much notice of, being taken aback by the horde of sovereigns. Sandra noticed the stamps were Victorian penny blacks and twopenny blues. So we now believe the rare stamps might be more valuable than the sovereigns."

"You may be wrong about the stamps being more valuable," said Mrs Neil. "My brother dabbled in rare coins for a number of years so I have some knowledge of their value. What condition were the sovereigns in when you took them out of the bag?"

Aunt Martha replied, "They were in excellent condition as if they had never left the bank."

"Well," said Mrs Neil, "these sovereigns would be classified as being in exceptionally fine condition. If so the sovereigns could be valued at over £2,000 and if you add that to the value of the rare stamps that would be quite a nest egg for Mr and Mrs Clark."

Next John and Sandra told Mrs Neil about the fire, and how the Craig brothers had poured petrol on a bonfire which caused the fire to spread to the woods. To cap it all, one of the brothers had hit John with an airgun pellet while he was running to the cottage to telephone for the fire brigade.

"Well, you certainly have had some adventures during your stay with your aunt. I am sure life will be a bit dull when you return to your home in Dunfermline. What with listening to all your stories, I had forgotten to bring out the cream cakes I prepared for you."

Saying that, Mrs Neil went away into the kitchen, made tea and brought it in with the cream cakes. John and Sandra soon ate them as they were hungry after telling her about their latest adventures.

As they had spent some time telling their stories Aunt Martha made their excuses to leave. "I shall telephone you next week and make arrangements to bring over some plants for your garden." Saying their goodbyes to Mrs Neil, John and Sandra left with Aunt Martha to return to the cottage.

23

John and Sandra's departure from Ladybank

The next day Sandra and John's father arrived in his Morris Minor, the car cleaned and polished as always. As he entered the cottage he was taken into the front room. After he was settled Sandra and John had to tell him about their latest adventure. He didn't know about the find in the old cottage or the woods being on fire as he had been away on business for a week.

He was taken aback at what they had experienced and said, "So many unusual things seem to happen to you when you are here. Although getting wounded with an airgun pellet must have been very worrying for your aunt."

After they had a meal together, Aunt Martha told John and Sandra to collect their suitcases they had already packed. Soon after they came downstairs the car was loaded up and John and Sandra made their farewells. This time their aunt was quite upset as she was close to them after nursing them through their illness and recuperation.

As Sandra and John got into the Morris Minor they looked up the road. There near the edge of the woods was a hare who seemed to be looking at them as they left.

Part Three

More Tales of the Brown Family

1

John and Sandra settle back in Dunfermline

On their return from Ladybank it took John and Sandra a day to settle back in their home at Dunfermline.

On the Monday they went back to their respective schools. It seemed strange to them after such a long break caused by their illnesses.

Over the next two weeks John and Sandra worked hard to catch up on the missed lessons at their schools. They even brought extra work home to help catch up more quickly. Their father helped them on some of the subjects.

Towards the end of the second week John and Sandra was asked by their father if they would like a break at the weekend. He had to see a fisherman at Dysart about some machine parts he had ordered and they could come along for the trip. John and Sandra readily agreed as they hadn't visited Dysart before.

So on the Saturday morning their father took them in his Morris Minor to Dysart. He took the coast road through Aberdour, Burntisland and Kirkcaldy.

On reaching Dysart, Mr Brown found the fisherman in one of the sheds in the port. While he was conducting his business, John and Sandra strolled around the harbour looking at the variety of fishing boats. Many of the boats had been lifted out of the water and onto the flat area above high water.

There were a number of men working on the boats. Some were cleaning the bottoms of their boats while others were repairing timbers and frames where their boats had been damaged. On one boat they could see two men securing a long plank in position, then riveting it in place with copper nail rivets and roes.

They could hear a constant hammering as the men drilled and riveted as they worked their way along the plank. As well Sandra and John could hear from a distance the echoing of the hammering off the high cliff above the harbour.

When he had finished his business their father strolled over to where John and Sandra were looking at the fishing boats. He suggested that they walk to the Ravenscraig Castle, which Sandra and John readily agreed to as they had seen enough of the harbour.

Together they left the harbour by the tunnel cut out of the rock at the far side of the harbour. Exiting from the tunnel they walked along a narrow beach to the wall surrounding the Ravenscraig Park. Walking further on, they approached a set of steps cut out of the surrounding rock. Their father told them, "These steps are famous as being the thirty-nine in number that inspired John Buchan to write his famous book *The Thirty-nine Steps*. As a boy with his brother in the 1880s the author played on these steps, which were close to where they lived. Their father was the Minister of the Free Church at Pathhead, which was across the road from the Ravenscraig Castle."

Hearing about the significance of these steps and its connection to the book, John was in a world of his own. He ran up and down the stone steps shouting, "I am a secret service agent escaping from the enemy."

He was on his fourth descent of the steps when he slipped and landed on his bottom in the very wet muddy grass at the foot of the steps. The only thing he injured with his fall was his pride but unfortunately it left him with well-soaked and dirty trousers.

Sandra and her father couldn't stop laughing when they saw the state John was in. His father said, "You can't blame anyone but yourself with rushing up and down those steps. Still, you're not hurt so we can now visit the castle.

After a walk around the castle with their father telling them the history of it they walked through the park. In the park they stopped to look at the aviary with its variety of birds. From the park they returned to Dysart harbour where the car was parked. Before he drove them back to Dunfermline John's father wrapped him in a blanket that he kept in the boot to stop the seat getting wet and stained. John in the back seat was quite glum.

His sister didn't say very much to John but it took her and their father quite an effort not to burst in laughter at seeing John's face.

On their return to Dunfermline their father meticulously checked, after removing the blanket, whether the back seat had been stained by John's wet trousers.

Inside their home, John changed his clothes and was soon back to his boisterous self, strutting around the house in his own dream world saying he was a secret service agent. Sandra just ignored him and went to her room and read a book until they were called for lunch.

2

The Brown family revisit Ladybank

On the Sunday Sandra and John suggested to their father that he telephone Aunt Martha and invite her to stay with them during the Christmas festivities. They had the previous week sent a combined letter to Aunt Martha thanking her for looking after them during their illness and recuperation period.

At first their father was reluctant to agree to their wishes, but gave in to them after they said that they would help prepare for the Christmas festivities.

When Mr Brown rang his sister that evening he was surprised when she agreed to stay with the Brown family over Christmas. She said that Christmas was a quiet time for her, being on her own. She added, "If your housekeeper wanted to spend some time with her own family I can prepare and cook the meals for you all over the holidays."

Her brother was pleased. "Your offer is most appreciated as I know my housekeeper likes to spend Christmas with her own family."

Before he rang off she said, "Would the children like to come to Ladybank next weekend? I have something to show them."

When he finished his telephone call to his sister he went into the lounge where Sandra and John were sitting reading books. He told them that Aunt Martha had agreed to stay with them over Christmas. Then he added that Aunt Martha had invited all of them to visit her next weekend as she had something to show them.

Sandra and John were delighted that Aunt Martha was coming to stay with them and readily agreed to her offer for them to visit her the next weekend. Sandra and John were puzzled about what Aunt Martha wanted to show them. Later their father called his sister back and said they would be coming to see her as suggested and should arrive at Ladybank early on the Friday evening.

During the week Sandra and John worked hard on their schoolwork to catch up on lessons they had previously missed with their illness. They didn't mind the hard work as the week went quickly with the anticipation of their visit to Aunt Martha the next weekend.

On the Friday evening Sandra and John were ready well before their father gathered his things for the trip. In the end they were urging him on to get ready quickly. He relented and soon had the car loaded up and they were on their way to Aunt Martha's cottage at Ladybank.

As they left Dunfermline the air was extremely cold and shaded areas on the way were covered in frost. When they approached Ladybank Mr Brown noticed that the road had become quite icy. He managed to come out of a couple of skids on the road into Ladybank. For the last part of the journey he drove more slowly to avoid skidding on the icy surface.

When they arrived at the cottage they could see the

road and pavement was covered in a heavy frost. The frost looked like a covering of sugar crystals as if many bags of sugar had been spread over the surface. As they walked up to the cottage the frost crunched under their feet.

Aunt Martha was at the door to welcome them and usher them into the cottage out of the cold night air. Once they had disposed of their cases she led them into the front room where she had a roaring log fire to warm them up after their cold journey.

After they had settled down she asked John and Sandra how they were faring at their schools. She added, "Your father, when he telephoned me, said that you had nearly caught up on the lessons you had missed."

Sandra said, "It's been hard work for John and me but we managed it by taking additional work home. Dad helped us on some of the subjects."

"That's good," said Aunt Martha. "You will be glad of the break this weekend."

3

Sandra is given a brooch by her aunt

The subject changed when Sandra said to her aunt, "You told Dad when he rang you that you had something to show us."

"Yes," said Aunt Martha. "Since I retired I've been going to classes for lapidary with my friend Mrs Neil."

"What is lapidary?" asked Sandra.

Her aunt replied, "It's the shaping and polishing of semi-precious stones. Recently there was a field trip to a hill near Cupar where there are agates that can be dug out. I managed to dig out some agate that had a light-brown lustre. At the class I was shown how to cut the stone and polish it. It turned out so well that I had it mounted in a brooch for you, Sandra."

With that Aunt Martha went upstairs and fetched the brooch and gave it to Sandra saying, "I know it is not your birthday until next week, but I would like you to have it now."

Sandra said, "Thank you very much, Aunt. I will appreciate it all the more because you prepared and polished the precious stone yourself."

John and his father asked to have a look at the brooch and admired Aunt Martha's handiwork.

Their father said, "You certainly brought out the colour with your polishing of the stone."

Aunt Martha then added, "I have one more thing to show you. Tomorrow if you are willing I want to take you to the old cottage of the Clark family. Tradesmen have been working on the cottage for several weeks and you should see the changes they have made to it."

4

The Brown family visit the old cottage

The next morning after breakfast the Browns put on their heavy coats and started to walk down to the Clarks' old cottage. Luckily the frost had melted away, the air having become warmer overnight.

On the way to the old cottage Sandra and John pointed out to their father where part of the woods had been destroyed because of the Craig brothers putting petrol on their bonfire, which had subsequently got out of hand.

When the family reached the old cottage they could see a number of tradesmen working on and in the cottage. As they entered the cottage one workman was connecting electric fittings and cabling to the junction box that had been fitted previously. Two bricklayers were extending the lean-to so that a bathroom could be installed. Another tradesman was knocking a hole in the lean-to wall so that a door could be fitted for entry to the new bathroom.

Sandra showed her father where the horde of sovereigns and rare stamps were found.

After a tour of the cottage and the garden Mr Brown asked his sister, "Will the old couple who lived in the cottage come back after the renovation of the property?"

She replied, "No, their son is going to sell the cottage for them and with what they get from the sale and the money from the sale of the sovereigns and stamps he will purchase a flat near his home in Glenrothes. He will ensure the flat is near the shops and have some neighbours close by for company."

Sandra asked her aunt, "What will happen to the old cooking range and other fittings? It will be a shame if they are scrapped with so much family history attached to them."

Aunt Martha replied, "Don't worry. The range and other fittings are to be preserved and fitted into an old cottage near Cupar. The cottage will be set up as it was in Victorian times so that the public can visit it." As they were leaving the old cottage she added, "If this old cottage could speak it would have many tales to tell us of the family's past."

The family walked slowly up the country road enjoying the warmth of the sunshine despite the cold weather. On their return to the cottage Aunt Martha made tea for everyone, which they all enjoyed after coming in from the cold air.

After their cups of tea Sandra asked her aunt if she would show her some of her other semi-precious stones she had done lapidary work on. Aunt Martha went upstairs and brought down a large box and showed Sandra, as well as John and their father who were also interested in her lapidary work on gemstones. Mr Brown said, "Now I can see what the cutting and polishing does to enhance the beauty of the stones." This they could see when comparing an uncut stone to a similar one that had been shaped and polished.

5

An unusual find in the woods

After a late lunch Aunt Martha said, "I have one more thing to show you, but it has to be later in the evening when I take you to see it." John and Sandra pestered her to tell them about what she planned for them to see, but she smiled and refused saying, "We will look at it when the rain goes off."

John and Sandra accepted Aunt Martha's refusal to explain the mystery so they went off to read their books in their rooms. In the meantime Mr Brown went out and bought a newspaper. On his return he settled down in the front room to read it while his sister did some sewing repairs on some clothes.

Later in the afternoon, their aunt, smiling with a mysterious look on her face, said, "Now it's time for us to walk to another part of the woods so that I can show you something unusual."

John and Sandra were quite excited, and, at last being able to resolve the mystery, put on their heavy coats as did Aunt Martha. The three of them managed to persuade Mr Brown to come along as well.

As the daylight was starting to fade their aunt took a

torch with her. After leaving the cottage she led them along a path separate to the one to the hollow tree. They continued on this path until they reached the far side of the woods where the land in front of them was a flat marsh. Aunt Martha told them to stop and said, "If we go any further our feet will sink in marshy ground."

While they were looking at the marsh their aunt shone her torch across the flat marsh. John and Sandra gasped as they could see pale flames on the surface. Sandra recovered from the surprise of seeing the flames and asked her aunt,. "What is causing the fames on the marsh?"

Her aunt replied, "It's a Will O Wisp or as some call it Jack O Lantern. The pale flames are caused by the spontaneous combustion of methane or other gases. The rotting down of vegetation below the marsh causes gases like methane to be formed."

While the others were watching the flaming over the marsh John being his adventurous self wandered over to where a knarled old tree had toppled over due to the recent storm. The shape of the old tree in the fading daylight had the shape of an old man crouched over the area where it lay as if it were protecting the spot.

John who always was looking for hidden treasure pulled aside a number of the broken branches of the crouching tree. What he saw made him step back in horror. There below the branches was the partial outline of a human skeleton.

He recovered and took a closer look at the skeleton. There seemed to be something attached to the skeletal hand. He stepped much closer and saw it was a badly worn leather pouch. He tried to lift it up but it was attached to the hand. After giving the bag a tug it came free.

With the pouch in his hand he shouted to the others, "See what I have found under the broken old tree."

The others came over and Mr Brown lifted the branches and saw the partial outline of the human skeleton. He turned to Aunt Martha who had come in behind him and said, "This find should be reported to the police – who knows when this person died or if it was under suspicious circumstances."

Now seeing the skeleton, Aunt Martha was somewhat disconcerted: "It's getting very dark and to me the air seems very creepy. We should return to the cottage." The others agreed with her as the darkness and the preserved skeleton gave an eerie and chilly feeling to the surroundings.

On their return to the cottage, John showed the rest of the family the pouch he had taken off the skeleton. Aunt Martha said, "Really you shouldn't have taken the pouch as it is evidence for the police investigation. When I go to the police station to report the find of the skeleton I shall hand it over."

Despite Aunt Martha's scolding, John opened up the worn leather pouch. In it there were two tools. After cleaning them with soapy water, John discovered that they were large bone needles. This excited John as he remembered the story that Mrs Neil had told them about the ancient weaver who went missing in the woods. He asked his aunt, "Do you think it's the skeleton of the weaver who may have been drowned in a bog accidentally or murdered by fellow weavers?"

His aunt answered, "Don't jump to conclusions because you have found a pouch containing bone needles. For all we know the skeleton could be quite recent in age.

Tomorrow we will walk out to the marsh area and get a better look at the skeleton and also pinpoint where it is in the wood. I wasn't sure in the dark where the site of skeleton is in the marsh. If I get the correct position of it I can give a better description to the police."

The next morning after their breakfast the Brown family walked to the woods. The path to the marshy area was quite damp as it had been raining most of the previous night, clearing by early morning.

When they reached the marsh area it took a while to find the knarled tree at the edge of the marsh. Mr Brown pulled back the branches of the tree to look at the skeleton. Now the full shape of the skeleton was revealed as the rain had washed the soil away from it.

He could see strips of cloth beside the skeleton which may have been the remains of its clothes. Mr Brown remarked to the others, "It is hard to tell how old the skeleton is as the marshy ground has preserved it in such a good condition. The police forensic section will examine it and from their tests they will decide the age of the skeleton."

With the others helping, Mr Brown placed broken branches from other trees around the skeleton to help hide it. Aunt Martha marked a large stone nearby with chalk to indicate the hiding place.

When they had finished they walked through the wood and back to the cottage. At the cottage Aunt Martha telephoned the police and gave them details of the hidden skeleton and its whereabouts in the woods. The policeman on duty said that he would pass the information on to his sergeant. He thought the sergeant would arrange to visit the site and take details of the skeleton. If she could visit the police station later that day and give a statement on the find in the woods, they would be grateful.

With that done the family relaxed and chatted in the front room with Aunt Martha avoiding any discussion about the finding of the skeleton. Later, she served up a meal which she had prepared the previous day.

After the meal Mr Brown said to John and Sandra, "It's time for us to return to Dunfermline, so collect your things and we will be off." John and Sandra collected their clothes from their bedrooms while their father chatted to Aunt Martha.

On coming downstairs, their father put all their suitcases in the boot of the car. Meanwhile John and Sandra said their farewells to Aunt Martha and thanked her for inviting them for the weekend. Mr Brown thanked his sister for her hospitality but said, "It was quite an eventful visit, what with seeing the Will O Wisp and then finding the skeleton in the marsh."

As Mr Brown prepared to drive away, John and Sandra waved from the back of the car to Aunt Martha standing on the front steps. As the car moved away Sandra looked back at the woods and was disappointed not to see a hare close by. Her brother said, "Never mind it would be too cold for the hare in this weather. He will be staying nice and warm in his nest on the bank in the woods."

Their father soon drove them back to their home in Dunfermline. On their arrival they were given cups of hot tea by the housekeeper as they were cold after the journey. Once they had their tea they had to tell the housekeeper about seeing the Will O Wisp and finding the skeleton in the marsh.

6

John gets a ride in a sports car

After an exciting weekend it was back to their respective schools for Sandra and John. At least they didn't have to work so hard or bring home extra work. They had in the previous week at last caught up on the missed lessons.

The only break from their school work was to relate to their respective classmates the unusual find of the skeleton after being shown the Will O Wisp with its unusual flames over the marsh.

On one evening during the week after finishing his course work John decided to walk around the garden. While in the garden he heard a loud tapping noise coming from the next door's garage. He knew the neighbours quite well, so out of curiosity he strolled around to their garage.

In the garage the neighbour Mr Graham was working on a car. John approached closer and noticed it was a two-seater sports car. The car was blue in colour with many chrome fittings.

John said hello and asked Mr Graham what firm had manufactured the car as he couldn't recognise the maker. Mr Graham replied, "I built it myself from a kit supplied.

It took me many months to build it, but it was worth it when it was finished."

Seeing that John was interested in the car he added, "Would you like a ride in the car? I was going to give it a run this evening."

John replied, "I'd love to but I will have to ask my dad if I can go with you."

John ran back to his home and burst into the lounge, breathlessly asking his father who was quietly reading a newspaper, "Mr Graham has built a sports car and has offered to give me a ride in it this evening. Is it all right for me to go with him, Dad?"

Mr Brown grinned at seeing John's excited state: "I knew Mr Graham was building a car from a kit. I've seen it a couple of times while he was building it. Yes, you can go with him if you have finished your homework."

John couldn't get out of the house quick enough when Mr Graham called for him.

Once John was in the car Mr Graham drove off on the road to Wellwood. He drove at a steady speed until they reached Wellwood. From Wellwood on the open road Mr Graham drove much faster but well within the speed limit.

John commented, "You drive much faster than my dad in his Morris Minor." Mr Graham laughed at John's remark as he knew John's father was a careful driver.

Mr Graham showed John how the car held the bends when going fast on the country road. At the approach to the Naval Stores at Lathalmond Mr Graham turned the car around and drove back to Dunfermline.

On their return John thanked Mr Graham for the ride

in his sports car. He said he was surprised what a small car could do.

When he was back home John was asked by his father, "Did you enjoy the ride in Mr Graham's car?

John replied, "Terrific. He went fast round bends so easily. I was surprised that a small car could go that fast."

The father laughed and said, "You should be impressed – the car is a racing model. Mr Graham has entered the car in one of the races at Knockhill next weekend."

John said, "Gosh! I had a ride in a real racing car."

The next evening Mr Graham knocked at the door and was invited in by Mr Brown. When he was settled in the lounge he took a book out of a wrapper. He said to Mr Brown, "This book gives a history of car racing. I thought your son John would like to read it."

Mr Brown said, "That's very kind of you. I shall shout for John to come in here wherever he is at the moment." He shouted for John and he came running down the stairs.

When he came into the lounge his father said to him, "Mr Graham has brought a book on the history of car racing for you to read."

John took the book and said, "Thank you very much, Mr Graham."

His father added, "I wouldn't mind reading it as well." After chatting for a while about racing cars Mr Graham left. Soon after John was off upstairs to read the book in his room.

For the next few days John would get his homework done early so that he could read the book on racing cars. By the end of the week he was going around the house pretending he was a racing driver competing with Niki Lauda. Sandra as usual just ignored him.

7

The Brown family get an invite to a race track

At the end of the week Mr Graham called on the Brown family again. He was invited in by Mr Brown and asked, "Have you come for your book?"

"No," replied Mr Graham. "I have come to ask you if you and your family would be interested in seeing the car racing at Knockhill next weekend? I have complimentary tickets. Would you be interested in going to the car racing? I have entered my sports car in the second event there."

Mr Brown called for John and Sandra to come downstairs and see him. When they came into the lounge their father said, "Mr Graham has kindly offered us three tickets for the car racing at Knockhill next weekend. He is racing his car there in one of the events. Would you like to go to it?"

Both together John and Sandra said, "Yes please."

Mr Brown was surprised to hear Sandra was just as keen as John was to go to the car racing at Knockhill. He said to Mr Graham, "Well that settles it, all three of us will go. Thank you for the tickets. We'll be cheering you on when your race comes up."

Before he left Mr Graham asked John how he was enjoying the book. He replied, "I have nearly finished it. Some of the photographs of the old races are excellent. Dad wants to read the book after I've finished."

Mr Graham said, "There is no hurry to get it back," and left to return to his home.

After Mr Graham had left John and Sandra were quite excited about going to Knockhill. They hadn't been to a car racing circuit before. They were still talking about it when they went to their beds that evening.

It seemed a long week for once waiting for the weekend to arrive so that they could go on their expedition. On the day of the racing, the Brown family saw Mr Graham drive his car off to Knockhill to register early for his race.

Later Mr Brown told John and Sandra to get ready to go as he wanted to avoid any problems with parking his car. In the end Mr Brown left a little late as John was not ready on time.

When they arrived at the stadium Mr Brown saw several Jaguars, a BMW and a Porsche already parked as well as other cars. Being embarrassed at driving an old Morris Minor car, he parked it in a corner a good distance away from the expensive cars.

From the car park they walked to the entrance and Mr Brown handed over the complimentary tickets. In the stadium their seats gave them a good view of the races.

The first race was quite exciting where the two lead cars were neck and neck for most of the race. The larger car won on the final straight coming into the finishing line.

The second race was more interesting as Mr Graham

had entered his car in this one. From the start, Mr Graham's car kept up with the leaders. Although he gained on the bends his car was not powerful enough on the straights.

The Brown family cheered Mr Graham every time he passed them. On one bend he was lucky to avoid two cars that crashed into barriers ahead of him but he had to slow down. The crowd seemed more excited with the crashes than the race.

With having to avoid the crashed cars, Mr Graham's car was overtaken and dropped back to be alongside the slower cars at the back.

After another lap Mr Graham started to get used to the track and pulled away from the slower cars. The crowd as well as the Browns, seeing that Mr Graham was starting to improve his position, cheered him on.

By the end of the next lap Mr Graham had caught up with the leading pack of cars. With the crowd urging him on, he made up on two of the cars in front of him. On the last lap Mr Graham was in fourth place and after taking the last bend just edged out the car in front of him and came in third place. Even though he was third the crowd gave him a great cheer when he reached the finishing line.

After he had reported in to the official and received his prize Mr Graham found the Brown family. Mr Brown patted him on the back and said, "You did well especially after the crashes held you back."

Mr Graham replied, "I felt inspired by the crowd cheering me on. So I had to make an effort to catch up with the leaders and the car responded well to enable me to get third place."

When the rest of the events were completed, the Brown

family walked out to the car park. Mr Brown drove them home.

A few days after the car racing John was walking up the road after getting off his school bus. He caught up with Sandra who had travelled on an earlier bus and was talking to a school friend. The two of them then walked the rest of the way to their home. As they approached the house John pointed out to his sister that there was a new car at their door. Sandra said, "I suppose Dad has the new car while the Morris Minor is being repaired. He did say he was getting engine trouble with the car."

As they reached the front door they saw their father at the window grinning at them, holding a set of keys in his hand. When they came into the lounge John and Sandra shouted, "Dad, don't tell us you've bought a new car."

Their father, still grinning, said, "Yes, I've bought a new Vauxhall Cavalier at a good price."

John then asked his father, "What have you done with the Morris Minor?"

"A chap who collects classic cars paid me a good price for the car as it was in such good condition."

That evening their father took them in the new car for a run out to the countryside and beyond and back to Dunfermline through Crossford. Sandra and John enjoyed the scenery of the countryside on the trip and the newness and smell of the leather covering on the seats.

The next day Mr Brown was outside the house when they came home from school, washing and polishing the new car. Sandra looked at John and said, "Nothing has changed, the car didn't need to be cleaned and polished!"

Later that evening their father took back the book lent

by Mr Graham to John, after reading it himself. He strolled down to the neighbour's garage where Mr Graham, with grease and oil covered all over his hands and arms, was bent over the engine. Mr Brown, seeing the state Mr Graham was in, put the book on a nearby shelf and said, "Thank you again for the tickets for Knockhill. The children and I enjoyed the experience. We would certainly go there again."

Looking at the state of Mr Graham's hands and arms, Mr Brown asked him, "What was wrong with the engine?"

"After travelling home from Knockhill I found that there was water leaking from the engine. On checking the engine in the garage I discovered that the cylinder head gasket had blown. So I am stripping it down so that I can fit a new gasket before I can drive it again."

At that point Mr Brown was glad to leave him saying, "I'll stick to the designing of my valves and pumps. Goodnight."

8

End of the school term

Despite missing so many lessons because of their illness John and Sandra did well in their term examinations. Sandra did better than John in English but John scored better in his mathematics examination.

At school John was nicknamed Jowe Brown as he could mimic the American actor Joe E Brown who acted in the film *Some Like it Hot,* which was having a revival on television. John to amuse his school friends used to mimic some of the teachers, but got detention when he was found out.

John was always looking for something different to do. One evening John asked his father if he could join the Scouts. His father was pleased with his son's request and said, "I will take you down to the Scout Hall on Friday. I know the Scout Master so I don't see any difficulty in getting you accepted."

On the Friday evening as promised Mr Brown took John down to the Scout Hall where he was introduced to the Scout Master, Mr Philips. He was quite pleased to take John into the group. The patrol John was put in had quite an unusual set of boys. One boy had long red hair and a freckled face. Another had short black spiky hair. The third one was tall and the remaining one was short and fat. Despite their differences in physical make-up, they got on well together.

The second time John went to the Scouts he and his patrol were shown something really useful. When he came back home from Scouts John told his father, "Tonight we were taught how to tie ropes with different knots." He went on to say, "We were shown how to tie reef, bowline and sheepshank knots."

John became quite expressive when he declared, "With knowing all these knots, I could tie up a burglar if he tried to steal from Aunt Martha's cottage and we caught him."

His father laughed and said, "You would have to get a strong man to hold him down first!"

The next week at the Scout Hall John, with his patrol, were shown the basics of first aid as well as being given details of how they could achieve certain badges.

Sandra on her part wasn't interested in joining the Brownies, but was chosen for the part of Mary Mother of Jesus in her school's nativity play. The school asked for help to build the scenery for the play. Sandra managed to persuade her father to build the structures for the set.

So, at the weekend, Mr Brown, who was good with his hands, went down to the school with Sandra. There he was given a plan of the set by the headmaster. In a store at the school there was plenty of plywood and planed timber that could be used to build the set.

As his business was quiet at that time Mr Brown spent several hours a day for the next few days on the building of the set. After marking out the outline of the set on the plywood and timber he soon had these cut to size to form the structure of the set. He had to get the help of one of the teachers to erect and secure the structure.

When he returned home after completing the set he told Sandra and John that they would be needed at the weekend to help paint parts of it. On the Saturday the Brown family put on their old clothes and went down to the school.

Mr Brown told Sandra and John what to paint on the set. Sandra was most careful with her painting but John in his boisterous way managed to slap the paint on the plywood. When he had finished, his clothes, hands and face were covered in it. Seeing him in such a state set Sandra and her father off in fits of laughter.

Mr Brown told John, "When you get home you may need some white spirit to get all that paint off your hands and face. Then you'll need to have a hot bath to get rid of the smell of paint on you."

John just grinned and said, "All right; I'll do that when I get home, but I enjoyed myself despite getting so much paint on me."

When the Brown family returned home Sandra and her father washed off the paint from their hands quite easily. For John it was a major job and he had to enlist the help of the housekeeper. When she first saw John as he came into the house she laughed and said, "John, you look as if you have been auditioning for a clown's job!"

It took several washes with soapy water to clean John's hands and face. After the first wash John's face looked as if he had smallpox with bits of paint still sticking to it. The next wash with plenty of scrubbing cleaned the rest of the paint off John's face. Although his face was clean it was quite red and puffy with all the scrubbing of it. John just sat there during all the face washes with a grin on his face.

9

A visit to the German market

On the Friday evening after the Brown family had helped to paint the scenery for the nativity play, Mr Brown suggested that they all visit the German market in Edinburgh on the Saturday. John and Sandra said, "Yes please, Dad."

Sandra added, "The girls in my class last week were talking about going with their parents to the German market."

"We can't go until the Saturday afternoon," said their father. "I have a design drawing to finish and need to post it to a firm on Saturday morning."

Early on Saturday morning Mr Brown was up early and putting the finishing touches on his pump design for his customer. After more than an hour of work he had a break and heard Sandra and John come downstairs. Looking over to them he noticed they were still in their pyjamas.

Seeing their father working on his drawings they went over to him and looked over his shoulder. Sandra looked at the design of the pump on the drawing and giggled: "The shape of the pump on your drawing looks like someone's bottom."

This made John roar with laughter though their father was not amused at first, but then he saw that Sandra was right and laughed with them.

Still not finished with his drawing Mr Brown said to the children, "Off you go and get dressed and have your breakfast while I finish my drawing."

When they had gone upstairs Mr Brown took another look at the pump and altered the shape of it on the drawing.

In the afternoon after lunch Mr Brown brought the Vauxhall Cavalier carefully out of the garage. He shouted for John and Sandra to come out as he would be driving to Inverkeithing Station where he would leave the car. Soon after John and Sandra came out of the house and climbed aboard. After they were in their father drove away. It didn't take him long to reach Inverkeithing Station where he parked the car.

Mr Brown bought return tickets for the three of them at the station and they waited for the train to Edinburgh. They only had to wait about ten minutes for the train but by then quite a large crowd were waiting for the same train.

The three of them managed to get seats together near the front of the second carriage. Just as they had got seated about a dozen young lads came into the compartment. Most of the youths had maroon-coloured tops on.

John asked his father why the youths were wearing the same tops. His father explained that they were Heart of Midlothian supporters on their way to the football match at Tynecastle in Edinburgh.

One of the group who seemed worse for drink started to stagger down the aisle. Luckily a tall youth who seemed to be the leader dragged him back by his collar and pushed him into his seat. Soon after the youth was fast asleep with his mouth wide open and snoring quite loudly.

John pointed out the sleeping youth to Sandra and their giggling started. Their father quickly told them to stop giggling at the youth's state. He added, "If the football supporters though you were making a fool of one of them there could be trouble." For the rest of the journey John and Sandra kept quiet and just admired the scenery on the way to Edinburgh.

At the other end of the carriage the football supporters were chattering away. Sometimes they would shout out a slogan about their team. When the train reached Haymarket Station the sleeper suddenly woke up and loudly shouted, "Where am I?" and got up. He was shuffled along by his leader and the rest of the group. On climbing onto the platform the football supporters started to sing their football songs as they made their way out of the station.

As the train left the station the carriage was now empty except for the Brown family; the compartment seemed strangely silent as the train went through the tunnel on its way to Waverley Station.

At Waverley Station the Brown family alighted from the train and walked out of the station and started to climb up the Waverley steps to Princes Street. As usual the wind was blowing quite fiercely down the steps.

Further up the steps, a lady with a big hat on was climbing up the steps desperately holding on to her hat. All of a sudden there was a gust of strong wind, which blew the lady's hat off her head. It bounced down the steps past the Brown family making their way up. Sandra, seeing the lady lose her hat, which blew past her, ran down the steps after it. She managed to pick it up before other people coming up the steps trod on it. She ran up the steps and handed the hat back to its owner.

The lady said, "Thank you so much for saving my beautiful hat. If you hadn't thought quickly to retrieve it the hat would have been damaged." After thanking Sandra, the lady ran up the steps with her hat in her hand. When she rejoined her father and John, Mr Brown said, "That's your good deed for the day done."

As they were only halfway up the long flight of steps they continued to the top. On coming out into Princes Street they could see all the stalls lined up along the street on the left-hand side.

The first stall was selling roasted chestnuts and Mr Brown bought some for Sandra and John. The next two stalls were selling sweetmeats and toffee apples. Further on there was a stall selling trinkets and curiosities made out of dark woods. Mr Brown told John and Sandra that they were made from woods in different parts of Africa. Next to the curios stall was a booth with a fortune teller. The next to last stall on the left-hand side was one selling wooden Swiss clocks and other wooden ornaments. Sandra saw a small wooden clock she liked as she approached the stall. Coming over to the stall she recognised the lady serving was the person who lost her hat on the Waverley steps.

The lady recognised Sandra and greeted her, saying, "How can I help you?"

Sandra asked her "What is the price of the small wooden clock?" pointing it out to her among the others. The lady said the price was three pounds but she could have it for two. Sandra, pleased at getting a discount, opened up her purse and paid for the clock. Her father, standing behind her, said, "Well now you have been rewarded for your good deed."

The last stall on the left-hand side was selling cups of hot chocolate. As it was cold weather their father bought three, which they all enjoyed.

After they had drank their hot chocolate their father said, "The stalls on the other side have similar products for sale as on the left so I don't see any point of going back to look at these stalls. I want to go to Jenners shop opposite and buy a silk scarf for Aunt Martha's Christmas present. You can look around to see if there is anything you may want to buy her as well."

In Jenners shop, after looking at several scarves on one counter, Mr Brown chose a silk scarf he thought would suit his sister. John and Sandra bought a small prettily shaped bottle of perfume for her.

With their purchases complete, their father said to them, "You must be hungry, I will take you up to the restaurant where we can have tea and cakes." As the restaurant was on the third floor Mr Brown took them over to where the lift was on that floor. On going up in the lift its exit was close to the restaurant.

In the restaurant Mr Brown found an empty table near one of the windows even though the restaurant was quite crowded with people. After sitting down he ordered tea and cakes for all of them. The waiter who served them quickly had their order placed at table. The three of them soon tucked into the cakes as they were hungry after walking in the cold weather.

Drinking their cups of tea they looked out of the window. The first thing they saw was the two-hundred-foot high Scotts Monument and the railway line running parallel to Princes Street. High above the railway line they could see the huge castle thrusting out from the volcanic outcrop of solid rock. In the distance they could see the hills with a snow covering on their tops. Mr Brown commented, "It's quite a sight from here, looking out over Edinburgh."

When they had finished their tea they made their way out of the shop down the Waverley Steps to the station. They didn't have to wait too long for their train to Inverkeithing. The train was quite quiet and Sandra and John slept for the whole of the journey. At Inverkeithing Station John and Sandra were gently woken up by their father.

On alighting from the train Mr Brown asked John and Sandra, "Would you like some fish and chips for your meal tonight?"

John and Sandra instantly said, "Yes, please!"

Mr Brown, once he'd picked up the car in the parking area, drove them to the square in Inverkeithing. After parking the car Mr Brown walked to the fish and chip shop. At the shop there was one person in front of him at the counter. She was asked by the assistant in a sing-song voice, "Do you want white pudden, red pudden, black pudden or haggis supper, hen?" The customer answered, "No thanks, I want twa pokes of chips and a fish supper, hen." The assistant duly dished up two bags of chips and one fish and chips. These she generously dosed with vinegar and salt which suited the customer. Then she wrapped the three items in used newspaper and handed it over after being paid.

Mr Brown was asked the same question by the assistant and said, "No thanks. I want three fish suppers but no salt or vinegar on them please." The assistant again supplied what was requested. Again she wrapped the fish and chips in used newspaper and after receiving the money handed them over.

Mr Brown walked back to the car where Sandra and John were patiently waiting for their meal. Their father said, "We won't be eating the fish and chips in my new car. You'll have to wait until we get home." So while their father drove back to Dunfermline Sandra and John were quite glum in the back, getting hungrier and hungrier. When they arrived back home the two children couldn't get the plates and cutlery out quick enough so that they could eat their fish and chips.

10

The Brown family visit Ladybank and see badgers

One evening after the visit to the German market Mr Brown said to John and Sandra, "I must telephone Aunt Martha about the arrangements for her coming to stay with us during the festive period."

Before he went to use the telephone Sandra said to her father, "Please Dad, will you persuade Aunt Martha to come to stay with us much earlier so that she can see me in the nativity play at the school?"

Her father replied, "I'll ask Aunt Martha if she could visit us early, but she may have made prior arrangements or perhaps have appointments for a doctor or a dentist."

Later that evening Mr Brown rang his sister. When she received his call she said, "It seems an age since you and the children visited me." When she was asked if she could make the start of her visit to Dunfermline earlier so that she could see the nativity play she was delighted. "My evening classes will be finished for the term and I don't have any appointments during that week." She paused: "If you didn't mind could you and the children come her for the weekend before my visit to your home? I have something to show them and Mrs Neil who they've been to see with me wanted to give them presents for Christmas."

Mr Brown smiled: "I'm sure John and Sandra would want to come for the weekend especially as they expect to experience something unusual in the woods these days!"

"Well that's settled," said his sister. "If you travel up to Ladybank early on the Friday and take me back with you to Dunfermline on the Sunday."

After ringing off, Mr Brown told John and Sandra about the proposed visit to their Aunt Martha's cottage and the reason to stay for the weekend. John and Sandra were delighted as going to Ladybank was always an adventure to them.

The weekend before the performance of the nativity play at Sandra's school, Mr Brown came home early from his office so that the family could travel to Ladybank shortly after Sandra and John came home from school.

Aunt Martha had said to her brother that they should travel to Ladybank as early as possible. She would have a hot meal ready for them on their arrival.

When he entered the house he shouted to Sandra and John, "Are you ready to go?" He expected them to be ready as they'd said that they would have their bags packed on the Thursday evening. John and Sandra shouted back from upstairs that they would be ready in a few minutes. After last minute throwings of extra things in their bags, John and Sandra came downstairs and waited at the front door while their father carefully brought out his car from the garage.

The drive was quite pleasant as the weather was mild

for December. The countryside on their journey looked quite stark with the trees bare. People walking on the sides of roads were still well wrapped up in dark clothes.

They arrived at the cottage in Ladybank by early evening. Aunt Martha must have heard the car coming up the road as they were greeted at the door by her.

Once they were settled in the cottage she sat them down in the kitchen. First she gave them soup and then traditional steak pie. Soon after having their meal they all sat down in the front room. Sandra turned to her aunt and said, "Well, Aunt Martha, what have you got to surprise us this time?"

Their aunt just laughed at the remark and told them, "Later this evening I am going to take you to a different part of the woods and show you where some badgers have a sett in a bank."

Sandra said, "That's great, but can't we go and see them now?"

Aunt Martha answered, "No, we will have to wait until it's late in the evening when they come out of their sett or hole in the bank. So you will have to be patient."

Changing the subject, she asked John and Sandra, "What's been happening to you of late?"

John got in first and told her how he had been taken for a ride in a new sports car. He went on to say, "The owner of the car gave all of us tickets for the racing circuit at Knockhill. We all went and saw Mr Graham the car owner compete in one of the races."

Next Sandra told her, "I was picked for the part of Mary mother of Jesus in my school's nativity play and Dad built the set for the play. John and I helped to paint the set."

"Well you have been busy," smiled their aunt.

Later in the evening Aunt Martha said to the rest of the family, "Get your coats on — we're going to see the badgers in the woods."

Mr Brown said, "Count me out. I shall stop and read the magazines I brought with me."

So off went the three of them into the woods carrying torches. Aunt Martha took a different path this time. On the far side of this part of the woods she stopped near a high earth bank. Near one of the holes in the bank she scattered some nuts and other food. She explained, "We must go back into the bushes away from the bank or the badgers will sense us and stay in their sett."

So they waited patiently for about twenty minutes before they heard a scraping of the earth. Their aunt shone her torch near the bank and there in front of the holes were two large badgers and two small ones eating the food and nuts.

Once they had eaten most of the food the two small badgers started to play. Aunt Martha shone the torch on the badgers to show John and Sandra how shiny the badgers' white and black fur was in the torch light.

She accidentally moved her torch so that the sudden movement of the light frightened the badgers and they scampered back into the hole.

Pleased with what they'd seen, the three of them made their way back through the woods. Passing near the marshy area brought back to John the memory of seeing the Will O Wisp and he asked his aunt, "Did you find out anything more about the skeleton we found in the marshy area?"

"Yes I did, but I will tell you about it when we get back to the cottage."

When they got back, Aunt Martha could hardly get her coat off before John pressed her again to tell them the latest news on the find of the skeleton. Mr Brown, hearing John's plea, added, "I'm curious to know about the latest news on the skeleton."

Amused at their eagerness to hear the latest news, Mr Brown's sister said, "Hold on, let's get settled in the front room before I bring you up to date."

Once the Brown family were settled, Aunt Martha related, "Once we reported the find of the skeleton, the police came out to the woods so I am told and carefully lifted the skeleton into a wooden box by placing canvas straps carefully under it. Then they slowly lifted it by the straps into the box. When they had removed the skeleton the police as a precaution examined the ground beneath. Just protruding from the ground below the skeleton they found a crucifix, which they put in a plastic bag to take away as evidence relating to the person who died.

"The box was taken away by the police and I believe transported to Edinburgh for forensic investigation. I heard from the local historian who was brought into the investigations after the Forensic Section's checks on the skeleton showed that the person had died in the mid-1500s. The historian was asked to find out where the crucifix came from originally.

"The Forensic Section in Edinburgh found out after cleaning the crucifix that it was made of an unusual stone and had an outline of a fish and the letter L carved on it. So you see the person didn't die recently and the possibility that it was the weaver in the old tale could still be true. If the historian gets any more information on the origin of the crucifix he will let me know."

After hearing what his aunt had to say about the skeleton John was impressed: "Gosh, that was so long ago it will be hard to find out any more about it."

John's father added, "That was quite interesting finding the crucifix. I am sure we would all like to hear if the historian unravels the mystery attached to it."

For the rest of the evening the family chatted about what they could do in the festive period while Aunt Martha stayed with them in Dunfermline.

11

Visits to the old cottage and Mrs Neil's home

The next morning Aunt Martha told the rest of the family she had to visit the old cottage and hand some keys over to one of the tradesmen working in the cottage. She suggested that the rest of the family could see the cottage now that it was nearly finished.

They agreed to what she suggested, and, after clearing up after breakfast, strolled down the country road to the old cottage. The walk was quite pleasant with the weather being so mild.

As they reached the cottage the Brown family were pleasantly surprised to see the whole of the cottage including the extension painted white and sparkling in the sunshine.

When they went inside they could see the interior was transformed. There was a beautiful bathroom set in the extension with a bath, washbasin and toilet with numerous cupboards fixed on the walls. All the rooms had central heating radiators and electric lights. The kitchen was so different with fitted units, an electric oven and dishwasher. The windows had been changed to ones with double glazing. All the interior walls were painted in pastel shades.

Mr Brown said, "From how you described the state of the original cottage layout in its Victorian state I'm amazed at the transformation of the whole of the cottage."

While the rest of the family were looking around the rooms, their aunt went over to the tradesman who was fitting panels over plumbing and electrical fittings and handed over a set of keys for the cottage. With this done the family walked back to Aunt Martha's cottage.

In the afternoon, just as Mr Brown and the children were settling down in the front room, Aunt Martha came out of the kitchen and said, "Let's be on our way to Mrs Neil's home." John and Sandra were quite happy to go but their father had to be persuaded to leave his magazines he was reading at his leisure. Aunt Martha said to her brother, "Would you mind taking your new car? I am curious to see what it drives like."

So they all got into the Vauxhall Cavalier. As Mr Brown was driving away his sister said, "You must drive this car much faster than the Morris Minor." Sandra and John in the back smiled and shook their heads. Their aunt smiled back and got the message as her brother gradually crawled up to fifty miles per hour on his way to Giffordtown!

As always Mrs Neil was pleased to see them when they arrived at her home. Aunt Martha introduced her brother to her as the family entered the house. Once they were settled in the front room Mrs Neil asked John and Sandra what they had been doing since she last saw them.

John and Sandra related to her the same stories about the sports car and the nativity play that they had told Aunt Martha about when they arrived at Ladybank.

After listening to their stories Mrs Neil was anxious to hear the latest information on the skeleton. Aunt Martha obliged and explained about the discovery of a crucifix with the skeleton.

When their aunt had finished her story Mrs Neil said, "That tale about a weaver being murdered may be truer than people gossip about, but the presence of a crucifix points to a religious man like a monk – not a weaver!"

At this point Mrs Neil fetched her famous cream cakes she had baked and brought them in with the tea. They all enjoyed the cream cakes, and John and Sandra had extra ones.

When they had finished and the table was cleared Mrs Neil brought out three Christmas-wrapped packages and gave the appropriate ones to John, Sandra and their aunt. She smiled: "You have to keep these and not open them up until Christmas Day."

As they had been there quite a while Aunt Martha got up from her chair and roused them all. "It's time to go." Just as they were leaving she took a Christmas-wrapped package out of a carrier bag she had brought with her and told Mrs Neil, "This is for you to open on Christmas Day."

As well as the package Aunt Martha handed over a set of keys to Mrs Neil and told her, "As we previously arranged these are the keys to my cottage, so that you can pop in from time to time while I'm away in Dunfermline."

As they left the Brown family wished Mrs Neil a Merry Christmas. Aunt Martha added, "I shall keep in touch while I am saying in Dunfermline."

12

Aunt Martha settles in at Dunfermline

On their return from Mrs Neil's home the Brown family spent a quiet evening together. While the others read books and magazines in the front room Aunt Martha finished packing her clothes and other accessories for her stay in Dunfermline.

After she had finished her packing she approached her brother and told him, "I hope you don't mind but as I will be staying away from the cottage for a long period I have arranged for any letters to be forwarded to me at your home."

Her brother replied, "That's fine – I think it's sensible because of your long stay."

The next morning John and Sandra loaded up the car while their aunt checked that she had locked all the windows and doors. She was especially thorough this time after her experience with the jewel thieves and because she'd be quite a distance away for such a long time.

The trip back to Dunfermline took about an hour. Once home the family were greeted by the housekeeper on their arrival, and Aunt Martha was introduced to Mrs Glover by Mr Brown as the family entered the house.

The housekeeper soon had them sitting down in the kitchen and provided them with hot soup and buttered rolls. Being a cold day the hot soup was most welcome. After they had finished lunch the housekeeper spoke to Mr Brown and said, "I have prepared an evening meal for you all that you can have at any time. As arranged, I shall go off in about an hour and travel to Edinburgh to stay with my relatives."

Later, as she was leaving, Mr Brown and the children gave her Christmas presents to take with her. They all wished her an enjoyable Christmas and would see her when she returned in the New Year.

In the evening Sandra and John persuaded their father and aunt to play Monopoly. As usual Sandra and John were very competitive and soon had first their father and then Aunt Martha out of the game. From then on it was fast and furious for the rest of the game with Sandra winning this time.

The next morning after breakfast their aunt picked up the local newspaper. On looking at the advertisements for films showing in the week at Dunfermline she said to the rest of the family, "I see the film *Chariots of Fire* is on at the local cinema. Would you like to see it this evening?"

"Yes please," chorused John and Sandra. Sandra added, "That's the film where they were acting a part of it on the beach in St Andrews which we watched on our visit there."

Mr Brown said, "Count me out: I have to finish a design drawing that's been outstanding for some time. I should try to finish it today. But the three of you should go to see it. The write-up on the film is very good."

That evening Aunt Martha took John and Sandra to the local cinema to see the film. As she had described it to them before, it was based on mainly two individuals who competed in the 1924 Olympic Games in Paris – Harold Abrahams, a Jew, running to prove himself in the face of the subtle hostility he found in his British environment and Eric Liddell a deeply religious man who refused to run on the Sabbath.

Partway through the film the scene the children had seen on the beach at St Andrews came up. John seeing it shouted, "There's the scene we saw at St Andrews where the actors were running on the beach."

Aunt Martha shushed him as people were looking around at them. John remembered where he was, blushed and kept quiet for the rest of the film, like Sandra became completely absorbed in it.

After coming out of the cinema Aunt Martha asked John and Sandra if they had enjoyed the film. John said, "It was great!"

Sandra said, "Yes, it was a good film; it was more special as we had experienced part of the playing of it at St Andrews." She added, "Eric Liddell must have been an unusual man with his religious belief and determination to win the longer race he was not originally picked for at the Olympic Games."

Their aunt said, "Yes, he was unusual and unfortunately died in a Japanese prisoner of war camp in World War II."

When they arrived home Mr Brown who had just finished his drawing work asked them, "How did you enjoy the film?"

"We all enjoyed it especially as we had seen the actors in the flesh on the beach at St Andrews."

That evening John and Sandra were quite content to go to bed early. Aunt Martha wondered later if John would be dreaming about running in the Olympic Games.

13

Preparations for Christmas

The following day Aunt Martha told the rest of the Brown family, "I've been neglecting doing my preparation for Christmas. I shall make a Christmas pudding and bake a cake too."

Her brother said, "Well, that's good of you. I'm free today so I shall take John and Sandra to play tenpin bowling at Rosyth. They often asked me to take them there. So we will leave you to it."

Soon afterwards they were on their way to Rosyth in the car leaving their aunt to get her cookery book out to start her preparations in the kitchen.

When they got there Mr Brown was able to park close to the entrance. Fortunately the bowling alley was not too busy so Mr Brown booked a rink right away. Once the ten pins were set up Mr Brown showed Sandra how to use the ball and she was able to knock some of the pins down each time.

John in his own blustering way bragged, "I know how to bowl, it's easy," but after bowling the balls down so badly that he didn't knock down one pin, he was embarrassed when the balls ended up in the side lanes.

At last he gave in and allowed his father to show him how to roll the ball with the correct grip. Now he was able to bowl better and stronger than Sandra. After a few goes John started to knock down numerous pins and sometimes got strikes.

When they had finished their session Mr Brown drove them back to Dunfermline. As soon as he got into the house John had to tell his aunt how he managed to get strikes with his bowling. His father added, "You didn't start very well so you shouldn't boast about your strikes at bowling."

Mr Brown seeing his sister's hands and face covered in flour said, "I can see you've been busy."

His sister replied, "Yes, I've made the Christmas pudding but I had to go to the supermarket to buy some ingredients for the Christmas cake."

Mr Brown gestured to his sister, "You sit down and I will make tea for all of us."

While they were drinking their tea there was a knock at the door. As Aunt Martha was nearest she opened the door to see who was there. The paper boy who was standing outside had a shock seeing her with flour on her face.

Looking over his aunt's shoulder, John said to the boy, "Don't be frightened; it's only my old auntie with flour on her face." The paper boy handed over the newspaper and ran off.

After John's remark there was silence. His father looked at him sternly, annoyed at his cheeky remark. Aunt Martha recovered and laughed and said to John, "For your cheeky remark you're going to do all the washing-up in the kitchen."

Saved by his aunt, John grinned. "All right, Aunt Martha, I will do the washing up," and he skipped into the kitchen.

14

A visit to the ancient part of Dunfermline

In the evening after Aunt Martha had finished her baking and John had washed up all the utensils and bowls used by his aunt in the kitchen the family settled down in the lounge.

Mr Brown said to his sister, "As I'm free tomorrow we should take a visit to the old part of Dunfermline. I know you haven't visited Dunfermline for many years so I thought it would be a nice change to visit the old part of the town and the Glen."

She replied, "Yes, I would like to go – it would bring back some happy memories of my youth."

The next day Mr Brown drove the family to the car park at the back of the City Hotel in Dunfermline. From there the family walked to the Abbots House which had walls coated in an unusual red colour; then on through the graveyard to the abbey by a side door.

In the abbey they looked around the building which was medieval in origin. Walking into the main part of the abbey, they came to the brass plate that covered the grave of Robert the Bruce, King of Scots. Mr Brown commented to John and Sandra, "I expect you've been told at school that the king's heart is buried at Melrose Abbey." The children nodded in agreement.

From the abbey they walked down the entrance steps to the start of the Glen. On the slope going in Sandra brought out from her pocket a bag of peanuts. She threw some of them down on the ground. Quickly out of the trees by the road scampered several squirrels. They soon had the nuts picked up. When Sandra threw some more nuts some pigeons came out of the trees and competed with the squirrels for the nuts. One pigeon was so bold as to snatch a nut out of the paws of a squirrel.

At the bottom of the road they came to the Glen Pavilion where there were five or six peacocks pruning themselves but they were frightened off when John and Sandra approached them.

Aunt Martha, looking through the glass door, pointed out the dance floor to them. She told them, "I had many a happy evening there when they held dinner dances. The men dressed in tuxedoes and ladies in their long dresses."

From the pavilion they headed towards the main Glen gates, passing the statue of Andrew Carnegie who donated the glen to the town.

As they came out of the entrance and walked along the street, a little girl who seemed to be with her father stepped off the pavement onto the road. Just at that moment a car came quite fast around the corner. John, being quick-witted, saw the little girl was in danger of being hit by the car so he jumped out and pulled the girl onto the pavement just as the car passed by.

The father of the little girl came up and thanked John

for preventing his daughter from getting injured. John was embarrassed: "It was nothing I was just able to see the danger quicker than anyone else."

When the rest of the Brown family caught up with John the father of the little girl had walked on. Mr Brown said, "Well done, John, you certainly acted quickly there to save that little girl from injury."

Taking another look at John, Mr Brown noticed that he had torn his trousers from scraping the pavement with his knees as he saved the little girl. He asked John, "Are you hurt?"

John replied, "No it's just a scratch on my knee." With the excitement over, the family headed for the City Hotel where Mr Brown bought the family lunch.

On their return to their house Aunt Martha told John, "Roll up your trouser leg. I want to see if you have a cut on your leg." When she looked at the cut on John's leg she could see it was not deep. She cleaned the knee with an antiseptic solution and covered the cut with a large plaster.

For the rest of the evening John made out the cut was worse than it was and started limping around the house. Despite making the others laugh his father told him off: "Don't be foolish – you only suffered a scratch on your leg!"

John quickly lost the limp on his leg.

15

John is injured while sledging

That night it started to snow heavily and it continued for the next two days. On the third day the weather was quite calm and the snow stopped falling, which allowed Mr Brown to clear the drive and nearby pavement of snow. He was soon busy with his spade.

With the snow so deep, John and Sandra built a snowman, making his face up with old potatoes and a carrot. Their aunt came to the door to see their snowman and was pelted with snowballs by John and Sandra.

When they went indoors John and Sandra asked their father if they could go sledging on the hill below Wellwood. Their father told them, "Yes you can go but the sledge I made for you last year is in the loft but I need to repair it as it was damaged." So while their father repaired the broken steel runners on the sledge John and Sandra helped Aunt Martha with her preparation for Christmas in the kitchen.

When he had finished repairing the sledge Mr Brown called for John and Sandra to get some warm clothes on. It only took minutes for them to get ready as their father put the sledge in the boot of the car. Aunt Martha declined to go with them as she said that she still had some preparations to finish for their Christmas dinner.

Mr Brown drove off with John and Sandra and after a short drive parked the car below the hill at Wellwood. When they got out of the car they could see there was plenty of snow lying there, enough to allow them to sledge.

There were a few children on the hill sledging but the hill was wide enough to take many more who wanted to sledge. Sandra and John had several goes on the sledge, each time coming down the hill to where their father was watching at the bottom.

Although Sandra took it easy sledging down the hill, John was always eager to go faster. So he took the sledge to the steepest part of the hill and further away from the main run. At the highest point John jumped onto the sledge and it went down the hill at quite a speed. At about halfway down it hit a stone and veered off to the left out of control, finally hitting the stone edge of an old well where the drift of snow had dislodged the protective cover. Disaster was to follow.

John tried to save himself but fell into the well, his leg catching the well wall at the top. Sandra nearby heard the crack of a bone and John crying out as he went down into the well. Running up to the well, she shouted to her father, "John's fallen into the old well...I think he's broken a leg."

Their father ran up the slope, slipping and slithering until he reached the well opening. Looking in, he yelled to John, "Can you move at all?"

John shouted up, "No, I'm in pain and I feel sick. I can't move my left leg."

Looking into the well, Mr Brown could see his son lying on the bottom, which looked like soft earth. He shouted to him again, "I'm going to get a blanket from the car so that you can wrap it around yourself to keep warm while I telephone for the fire brigade."

On his return, he dropped the blanket into the well for John to catch. This done he said to Sandra, "Keep talking to John while I go down and telephone the emergency services."

Again Mr Brown slipped and slithered down the slope. When he got to the bottom, he ran to the nearest telephone box which had been vandalised! After cursing the absent vandals he ran on down the road.

Next he approached the first house that had a car outside and knocked on the door. An old lady opened it and asked him what he wanted. Drawing breath, Mr Brown explained to her that his son, while sledging, had fallen down the old well near the bottom of the nearby hill.

The old lady, seeing his distress, invited him in and showed him where the telephone was in the hall. He quickly rang the emergency services, explaining the plight of his son. With that done, he made his way back to where Sandra was keeping up a conversation with her brother, now wrapped tightly in the blanket trying to keep warm.

When he reached the opening of the well Mr Brown shouted down to his son, "John, the fire brigade should be on their way to rescue you by now."

Ten minutes later the fire tender arrived, followed shortly afterwards by an ambulance.

The firemen took ropes and harnesses out of the tender and climbed up to the well. They dropped a rope down into the well and tied the end to a nearby tree. One of the firemen carrying a harness lowered himself on the rope to the bottom of the well.

At the bottom he checked how John was faring and found, with his aid, he was able to stand up although with much pain from his broken leg.

The fireman fitted the harness on to John and the two firemen above gradually lifted John out of the well. The fireman supported the poor boy as he was raised, then climbed up the rope himself. Once John was lifted out of the well, the attendants from the ambulance laid him on a stretcher and took him down to the road.

At the ambulance Mr Brown gave the attendants details of his son and his injury. The driver said he was taking his son to the West Fife Hospital in Dunfermline. Hearing where he was being taken he said, "I will have to pick up my sister near here but then I will drive the family to the hospital."

With Sandra beside him, Mr Brown drove back to their home. Getting out of the car, leaving Sandra, he quickly went into the house and told his sister what had happened to John and that he was injured and being taken by ambulance to the hospital.

"I'll get my coat on and come with you." Aunt Martha was shocked. As soon as she was in the car her brother drove off quite fast, which was unusual for him.

Arriving at the hospital, Mr Brown made enquiries about his son at the reception desk. A nurse was called for by the receptionist and she came out to see the Brown family while they were waiting. She told Mr Brown, "Your son has been taken to the operating theatre so that the surgeon can reset his broken leg. Once this is done, they'll put his leg in plaster. He should be taken back to a ward in about an hour's time. I'll get you some tea while you're waiting for your son to be moved to the ward."

After what seemed a long wait the nurse returned and led the family to the ward where John had been moved to from the operating theatre.

When the family sat beside him they could see he was still under the effects of the anaesthetic. His father asked him how he was after the operation. John, still dazed, murmured, "I'm all right, Dad, I just want to sleep now." All the family wished him a speedy recovery and left him to sleep!

The next day the Brown family visited John in the same ward of the hospital. He seemed much better but was still taking painkillers because of the operation on the broken leg. He showed them the plaster and where other patients had signed their names. Sandra had to add her name on the plaster.

By the end of the week Mr Brown again visited the hospital to see the surgeon about John's progress. In the ward the surgeon told him that the leg-break was knitting quite well and John could go home with him. He added that he could use the crutches to walk around the house and garden but should not overdo the walking as the bones were still healing. All being well the plaster would be removed early in January.

So John came back to his home, receiving a welcome from his aunt and sister, glad not to have to stay in hospital over the Christmas period.

16

The family celebrate Christmas

With the family involved in visits to the hospital to see John, the preparations for Christmas had still to be finished. The Christmas tree that Mr Brown had brought home and set up in the lounge still had to be decorated.

Aunt Martha and Sandra soon had this in hand – streamers all over it and then baubles and chocolates on it. Finally lights were fitted and these, when tried, lit up without having to change bulbs or a fuse.

John, who had been reading *Treasure Island* again, came down dressed like the character in the book, Long John Silver. He had borrowed his father's black jacket, which came down below his knees, and on his head wore an old hat. For the final touch he had cut out the shape of a parrot and painted it, which he pinned onto his shoulder. So while his aunt and Sandra were finishing off the Christmas decorations John with his crutch stumped around and voiced plenty of "aaarr"s in his impersonation of Long John Silver! At least it made his aunt and Sandra laugh. When he had finished they pelted him with soft spare baubles.

On Christmas Eve one by one the members of the

Brown family hid their presents under the Christmas tree. That evening the family sat in the lounge quite happy to be together to celebrate Christmas. With all the preparations complete, including their needs for the Christmas dinner, the family went to their beds early.

On Christmas Day all the family were up early, except for John who was left to lie in as he was still feeling the effects of his injury. When he did come down wearing shorts (for they allowed him to dress himself) they ate a late breakfast Aunt Martha had cooked. After breakfast they went into the lounge and sat near the Christmas tree, John in an easy chair with his plastered leg supported on a cushion.

So, one by one, the Christmas presents were given out. Their aunt had a silk scarf and novels from her brother. John and Sandra gave her a book on lapidary. John and Sandra had books from their father and knitted jumpers from Aunt Martha. The father received a set of pens from John and Sandra and a coloured waistcoat from his sister. When they had finished opening their presents the floor was covered in coloured wrapping paper, which was quickly gathered up and tidied away by Aunt Martha.

John and Sandra started to try on their jumpers. First John couldn't get his jumper beyond his shoulders no matter how hard he tried. Sandra being much smaller than John found her jumper was too big and it sagged over her shoulders and extended down to her knees. Aunt Martha and their father couldn't help laughing at their difficulty. Aunt Martha smiled: "I think you've got the wrong jumper, Sandra – you have John's jumper and John has yours. I know what's happened. I noticed that the labels had fallen off your presents so you've picked up each other's present by mistake." So it was easily solved, with John and Sandra exchanging jumpers, and this time they filled them quite neatly.

Later in the day preparations were made for Christmas dinner. When Mr Brown and the children were sat down in the dining room Aunt Martha brought in the cooked turkey, stuffing and roast potatoes, which they all enjoyed. This was followed by a hot Christmas pudding which they had with cream.

When they had finished they retired to the lounge to rest after such a large meal. John who hadn't eaten much since his injury groaned. "I am stuffed, that was a great meal, Aunt Martha." The others agreed that she had cooked a splendid Christmas dinner.

After they had been resting in the lounge for about an hour, their aunt went to her room and brought down two letters and a package.

She said to the children, "I have two letters that will be of interest to you." She took the first one out as she went on to explain, "This is a letter from my friend, Mr Reid the historian, whom you met at Ladybank. There is to be an exhibition of Pictish and Iron Age artefacts at Cupar next spring and you will be officially invited to it. In the second part of the letter he tells me that a solution to the identity of the skeleton you found has been found. He did quite a lot of research on the origin of the skeleton. This was solved when he visited the curator at Falkland Palace. The curator after some delving came upon details of records from the Lindores Abbey written by the monks in the 1500s. In these records he found that a weaver called

Crispin, also a religious man, was given the special crucifix by them for all the help he had given the abbey in supplying cloth and selling their fruit which the abbey was famous for in the area. The weaver who was a constant visitor to the abbey was believed to have been murdered but the abbot could not prove who did it.

"The second letter is from Mr Clark, the son of the old couple that owned the old cottage at Ladybank. His own wife cannot have children so with such a considerable amount of money being realised from the sale of the gold coins and rare stamps he has with me as the executor put into a trust £1,000 for each of you for your future education."

Mr Brown, on hearing what the letter contained said to his sister, "That was a very generous gift from Mr Clark. I must write and thank him. As regards the skeleton, discovering the identity of the person was quite a revelation."

Finally Aunt Martha unwrapped the package and brought out a framed photograph of a hare taken in the Lower Woods in Ladybank. After handing it over to John and Sandra, she said, "I hope you will put this framed photograph on your mantelpiece. The photograph will remind you of the times when you contributed to the unravelling of the mysteries of the Ladybank Woods and the secret of the old cottage."